My Life as a Coder

Other Books by Janet Tashjian
Illustrated by Jake Tashjian

The My Life Series:
My Life as a Book
My Life as a Stuntboy
My Life as a Cartoonist
My Life as a Joke
My Life as a Gamer
My Life as a Ninja
My Life as a Youtuber
My Life as a Meme

The Einstein the Class Hamster Series:
Einstein the Class Hamster
Einstein the Class Hamster and the Very Real Game Show
Einstein the Class Hamster Saves the Library

By Janet Tashjian

The Marty Frye, Private Eye Series:
Marty Frye, Private Eye: The Case of the Missing Action Figure
Marty Frye, Private Eye: The Case of the Stolen Poodle
Marty Frye, Private Eye: The Case of the Busted Video Games

The Sticker Girl Series:
Sticker Girl
Sticker Girl Rules the School
Sticker Girl and the Cupcake Challenge

The Larry Series:
The Gospel According to Larry
Vote for Larry
Larry and the Meaning of Life

Fault Line
For What It's Worth
Multiple Choice
Tru Confessions

JANET TASHJIAN

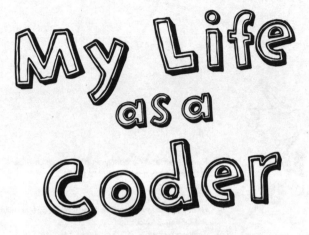

My Life as a Coder

with cartoons by
JAKE TASHJIAN

Christy Ottaviano Books
Henry Holt and Company

Henry Holt and Company, *Publishers since 1866*
120 Broadway, New York, NY 10271
mackids.com

Our books may be purchased in bulk for promotional,
educational, or business use. Please contact your local
bookseller or the Macmillan Corporate and Premium Sales
Department at (800) 221-7945 ext. 5442 or by email at
MacmillanSpecialMarkets@macmillan.com.

Library of Congress Control Number: 2019941041

First edition, 2020

Printed in the United States of America by
LSC Communications, Harrisonburg, Virginia

ISBN 978-1-250-26179-3 (hardcover)
10 9 8 7 6 5 4 3 2 1

ISBN 978-1-250-75964-1 (international edition)
10 9 8 7 6 5 4 3 2 1

For Jackson

My Life as a Coder

THANK YOU??

I DOUBT THEY'D EVER TEACH THIS in science class, but there HAS to be some connection between how much fun you had on a long weekend and how excruciating it is to go back to school afterward.

Matt and I spend Tuesday limping to our classrooms like wounded soldiers on a battlefield. He occasionally stops and doubles

battlefield

over. "I'm not gonna make it," he cries. "Go on without me!"

For the past few months, Matt and I have been obsessed with comedy. We follow a ton of comedians on Instagram, and for several nights we've stayed up past midnight laughing at their hilarious stories.

Matt's always been a jokester and I'm pretty good at concocting ridiculous schemes, so we're convinced we're destined to become the next famous comedy duo.

When I finally get home from that grueling day back, I'm surprised my parents are already there. Dad's been logging long hours storyboarding for the film he's working on, and Mom must've had a shortened day because she's in a T-shirt and leggings instead of her usual scrubs.

logging

shortened

They follow me into the kitchen as I walk in to grab a snack. The goofy smiles on both their faces make me uneasy. Before I can ask what's going on, Dad speaks up.

"We've got a surprise for you!" He points to a corrugated cardboard box on the kitchen table.

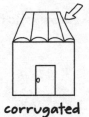

corrugated

I haven't gotten any good grades lately and it's nowhere near my birthday, so I'm curious to see what's inside.

Before I can open it, however, Mom puts her hand on my shoulder. "You know how we've had con-versations about the importance of learning new things?" she asks.

Suddenly the prospect of this gift seems a lot less appealing. I nod and reach for the box once more but Mom stops me again.

appealing

neuroplasticity

"Your brain is still developing, so it's important to keep giving it new tasks," Dad adds. "It's called neuroplasticity."

Case closed; this present is definitely NOT something cool. I decide whatever it is can wait until after I've finished an entire bag of Goldfish.

"I just walked in the door and you're already talking about stuff I don't understand." I point to the box on the table and tell them whatever it is, I'm no longer interested.

"That's too bad," Mom says, "because it's something you've wanted for a long time."

You have my attention!

intrigued

Her comment has me intrigued. I wipe the Goldfish crumbs off the counter and sit down. I remember the conversation we had a few months ago when Carly took a class in Mandarin; my parents tried to talk me into taking it with her to "expand my brain" but I told them I'd like to get an A in my own language first before studying a new one.

"We've been impressed with the computer science work Umberto's been doing," Mom continues. "It seems like you have been too."

"Umberto's a brainiac," I tell them. "I can beat him at video games and I'm good at finding the perfect meme for any situation, but he's a thousand times better at actual programming."

programming

"Well, maybe that's because you've never tried." Dad pushes the box toward me and I slowly open it.

Inside is a laptop!

laptop

illuminates

applications

"No way, my very own computer! Now I won't have to borrow yours all the time."

When I press the power button, the screen immediately illuminates. AWESOME! It boots up in lightning speed, but I'm confused by the empty screen.

"The desktop's empty. Where are the games and applications?" I say.

"That's the beauty of it," Dad says. "It's only got a word processing application for schoolwork. The rest of the applications you'll have to write yourself."

"WHAT?!" I shout. "I don't know how to code!"

"Yet!" Dad adds. "We got the email on the upcoming after-school programs. There's a coding elective starting in a few weeks—that's why we're giving this to you now instead of waiting for your birthday."

My father may be the one talking, but this scheme to get me to do more work has Mom's name all over it.

"The whole point of an elective is that it's something I choose," I whine. "I was going to take the comedy after-school class, not computer programming!"

"You can sign up for both." Mom separates her hands like she's showing off a giant bass she just caught. "It's all about expanding your brain."

I thank them for the computer and head upstairs. As soon as I'm in my room, I'll download all the games and applications I want. Who ever heard of creating and designing your own fun? What is this—the Middle Ages?

On my bed I scoot next to my dog, Bodi, and open the laptop. I can't complain, really. The design is sleek and the keyboard is comfortable. But when I try to access the Internet, I can't find our home network anywhere.

sleek

"You looking for the network?" Dad sticks his head into my room. "We thought it would help you stay focused if you weren't distracted by the Internet, so we had the store take out the wireless card."

wireless

My parents have absolutely lost their minds. "WHAT GOOD IS A LAPTOP WITHOUT WI-FI??" I shout.

"I guess you'll find out," Dad laughs as he heads down the hall.

It's official, my parents have gone

berserk. I stare at my new laptop, a piece of technology as effective as a bag of rocks.

A present that makes you work isn't a present at all.

WORST. GIFT. EVER.

AT LEAST
UMBERTO'S HAPPY

abacus

archaic

AT MY LOCKER THE NEXT MORNING, Matt thinks my new laptop without Wi-Fi or applications is the stupidest thing he's ever seen. "They might as well have given you an abacus!" he says. "Talk about archaic!"

Carly, of course, agrees with my parents and takes their point further by adding her two cents on brain plasticity. "That's why people can recover after strokes or brain injuries," she says. "Our brains are actually incredible machines."

"Speak for yourself," I say. "All mine's ever done is get me in trouble."

"You're looking at this all wrong," Umberto tells me. "You're holding the key to the universe! You love the programs I've written. You can program that baby to do ANYTHING!"

I wish his enthusiasm were contagious.

contagious

"Yeah, let's ALL sign up for the coding class," Matt suggests. "Let's sit there for an hour after school and realize there's tons of stuff we still don't know."

numbskull

"Don't be a numbskull," Carly says. "Let's hope you haven't finished learning new things at twelve years old." When she smiles, I spot a sliver of apple on one of the wires of her braces. I run my own tongue over my teeth and Carly takes the hint. She checks the mirror she always carries in her bag and removes the food before anyone—mostly Matt— can tease her about it.

"Well, I'm signed up," Umberto says. "Even if I already know some of the material, the class is free, so I'm taking it."

"What about comedy class?" Matt asks me. "You still in?"

Carly pulls up the schedule on her phone. "I was thinking of signing up for the comedy class too," she says.

"Great," Matt answers. "That class will definitely need audience members."

"I can be funny!" Carly says.

Matt rolls his eyes. "Sure you can."

"The coding class and comedy workshop are both Thursday afternoons." Carly looks over at me. "I guess you can only take one."

I shake my head and walk to first period. Isn't school serious ENOUGH? Electives are supposed to be fun—not more academic drudgery. Which class should I take?

drudgery

Ms. McCoddle flashes maps on the Smartboard as we take our seats. We just finished studying the civilization of Ancient India, now it's on to Mesopotamia. My mind can't stop repeating *Mesopotamia. Mesopotamia. Mesopotamia.* Ms. McCoddle is talking about how the country no longer exists but was located in present-day Iraq. However, all I keep thinking about is

civilization

how *Mesopotamia* would be a great name for a cartoon character who's a slob.

"One of the most important inventions of all time—the wheel—was created in Mesopotamia," Ms. McCoddle continues. "Wheels were initially created to make pottery—it took three centuries before someone realized you could actually attach wheels to a chariot."

chariot

Three centuries is probably how long it'll take me to figure out how to use my new laptop. Maybe I SHOULD take that coding elective. I doodle in the margins of my notebook—a Mesopotamian making stupid clay bowls not realizing he could be racing through town in a tricked-out wagon instead.

The room suddenly feels quiet;

I look up and notice half the class—including Ms. McCoddle—staring at me.

"Derek, do you remember from the reading what kind of religion was practiced there?" Ms. McCoddle asks.

First of all, the words *remember* and *reading* hardly ever go hand in hand when you're talking about me. Reading is still my worst subject, no matter how hard I try. Second of all, I didn't even know we HAD a reading assignment due today.

I decide to follow my usual strategy: When in doubt, guess.

"Uhm...Scientology?"

When Ms. McCoddle closes her eyes, I realize my answer is a giant misfire.

"Only in L.A.," she says. Her

misfire

polytheist

comment explains nothing, yet kind of explains everything.

"Mesopotamia was a polytheist society—who knows what that means?" Ms. McCoddle turns away from me as if I might contaminate this answer too.

"It means they worshipped multiple gods, not just one," Umberto answers.

"Exactly," Ms. McCoddle says.

I slump in my seat and put my head down. If Umberto being right and me being wrong is how coding class is going to go too, I might as well throw in the towel now.

FINGERS CROSSED

FOR SOME UNEXPLAINABLE REASON, there's a ton of homework this week. A three-page paper on agricultural societies, a math worksheet on parallelograms, and an oral presentation for media studies. WHAT IS GOING ON?! The second I get home from school, I know what I have to do: Procrastinate. Procrastinate HARD.

unexplainable

agricultural

parallelograms

Dad's working in his office downstairs, which means I can't watch TV in the family room. Luckily, the world is at my fingertips because I have my phone.

I climb onto my bed with a sleeve of Oreos and Bodi. I know chocolate can be harmful for dogs—duh—but no one's ever said dogs can't lick the creamy inside of an Oreo. I crumple up the wrapper and try to hit the ceiling. I watch a video of a raccoon sneaking into someone's house through the doggy door. I make a tower out of all my sneakers, then knock it over with my backpack. I lie on my bed and rub Bodi's belly.

All of that takes less than fifteen minutes—what am I supposed to do NOW? (Don't say homework.)

Matt must also be procrastinating

because he starts texting me memes, GIFs, and videos one after another. Not responding would be rude, so I text back a string of my own favorites for him to enjoy. Making time for friends is important, right?

Still feeling amicable, I text Carly too. She probably finished her homework on the bus and is already relaxing, giving herself a manicure or something. So I'm surprised when she texts me back a row of grimacing emojis. And even more surprised when she calls instead of texts.

"Look, Carly, I'll have to call you back. Some of us are busy procrastinating."

"I haven't gotten any work done today!" she begins. "I don't know what's wrong with me."

amicable

manicure

"Nothing's wrong with you," I answer. "You're finally acting NORMAL."

"I don't feel normal," she continues. "I feel so anxious all the time."

I don't want to bring it up, but I wonder if these new feelings have anything to do with the wildfires and evacuation we had a few months ago. Carly was so concerned about natural disasters and rescue animals that she barely slept. She's not worried about another tragedy, is she?

Carly and I talk for a few more minutes. I try to calm her down by mentioning Princess Poufy, the extravagant Pomeranian we had to take care of during the fires, but eventually she gets upset that she's

tragedy

★ 20

wasting time on the phone instead of being productive. We hang up to do our homework—or at least that's what we tell each other.

To be honest, Carly has seemed a little off lately. When we did the module called Mental, Emotional, and Social Health in Ms. Miller's class a few weeks ago, I had a twinge of recognition when we discussed the symptoms of depression. Carly's always taken things more seriously than the rest of my friends, but lately she's blaming herself for mistakes instead of just trying to move on. It also seems like she's having trouble concentrating and has been especially sensitive. She actually said she felt worthless when she got a B-minus on her English paper, a grade I would KILL

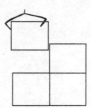

module

symptoms

worthless

for. I'm not overly worried about Carly—just a bit concerned.

Mom sticks her head into my room to see how my homework's coming. I lie and tell her I'm almost done.

"Excited for coding class tomorrow?" she asks.

"I'll be the stupidest person there," I answer.

"So it'll be familiar territory, right?"

territory

Just as I'm about to get mad at her for being insensitive, I realize she's kidding and shoot her a fake laugh instead.

insensitive

"You're creative," she says. "You might take to it naturally." She tilts her head and smiles. "One thing's for sure—you won't know until you try."

Yes, she's my mom and HAS to say stuff like that, but she really seems to believe I might be good at this whole programming thing. She's pretty smart, so I guess it's POSSIBLE she might be right. Her faith in my ability to master something new almost makes me want to get cracking on my homework.

Almost.

WAIT, WHAT?

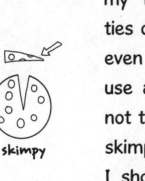

skimpy

THE GOOD NEWS IS I ACE MY math homework; the bad news is my report on agricultural societies only ends up being one page— even after I double-space it and use a larger font. Ms. McCoddle's not too pleased when she eyes my skimpy paper. I guess in hindsight, I should've started my homework earlier instead of watching comedy videos.

When I finally get to coding class at the end of the day, I'm surprised at how full the room is. Umberto's already there, notebook and pen raring to go. My plan was to sit next to him, but the only empty seat is in the first row.

Umberto gives me a grin and a thumbs-up. I roll my eyes and shuffle to the front. This is going to be a VERY long fifty minutes.

I plop beside a girl I've never seen before. She's wearing black jeans, a black AC/DC T-shirt, and boots—even though it's eighty degrees outside. Her wrist is covered with the plastic bands you get at hospitals.

I gesture toward her arm. "You go to the emergency room a lot?"

She looks at me like I just asked the dumbest question of all time. "It's a fashion statement."

"I didn't know they sold designer hospital bracelets."

"I live near the hospital—people throw them away as soon as they get outside."

"So...you go through the trash can outside the hospital? Isn't that a biohazard risk?" Who IS this girl?

biohazard

"I add LED lights to the bands, then program them to blink randomly." She shakes her wrist and a string of lights flash on and off.

Before I can tell her how cool that is, a voice booms from the doorway. "Welcome to coding class!"

It takes me a few seconds to place where the voice is coming from.

"Hi, Ms. Felix!" Umberto waves.

Odd, the only Ms. Felix I know is the lunch server...

Sure enough, the woman walking to the front of the room is the person who serves us tater tots. Without her apron and hairnet, she looks like a regular grandmother. What is she doing teaching programming?

"For those of you who are surprised to see me without a spatula in my hand, I have a degree in computer science and do consulting on the side. Just like you, I have a life outside this school."

consulting

A few kids laugh, but I'm too discombobulated to join in. It's like that time the door to the teachers' lounge was open and I spotted Ms. McCoddle scrolling through her phone while eating a Big Mac. Am I the only one who doesn't want to see the behind-the-scenes lives of teachers? Or lunch servers?

discombobulated

$$X1 \leftarrow (c+h)2(3 \times a)$$

algorithm

"Actually, there are some real similarities between cooking lunch and programming," Ms. Felix continues. "In coding, you write an algorithm that is very much like a recipe you'd use in cooking. The instructions you follow in a recipe are similar to the step-by-step directions you'll be writing for your computers."

I'm sure if I sat here long enough, I'd come up with a few connections between my laptop and a Sloppy Joe but I'm still trying to wrap my head around Ms. Felix as a computer guru. My dad always talks about how important it is to think outside the box—I guess this is an example of expanding the possibilities of how the world can work.

"Since we're talking about recipes, let's start with creating an algorithm for chocolate chip cookies," Ms. Felix says.

"You brought some with you, right?" Umberto teases. He's always been on the good side of all the lunch servers, a smart move if you're interested in larger portions—and who isn't?

Ms. Felix draws a series of connected blocks on the board.

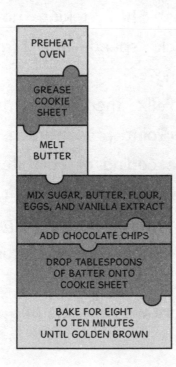

PREHEAT OVEN

GREASE COOKIE SHEET

MELT BUTTER

MIX SUGAR, BUTTER, FLOUR, EGGS, AND VANILLA EXTRACT

ADD CHOCOLATE CHIPS

DROP TABLESPOONS OF BATTER ONTO COOKIE SHEET

BAKE FOR EIGHT TO TEN MINUTES UNTIL GOLDEN BROWN

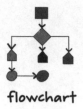
flowchart

When she's done, the Smartboard is covered with a flowchart of all the steps except the most important one—EATING these imaginary cookies. I'm glad we don't have more lunch servers teaching classes; if their methods are anything like Ms. Felix's, I'd be hungry 24/7.

I sneak a peek at the new girl in black. She's taking notes at breakneck speed—am I missing something?

Ms. Felix then whips through a PowerPoint presentation, which uses the coding of Fortnite as an example. Smart. It's no comedy class, but maybe learning to program my new laptop won't be as torturous as I thought.

"Before we conclude this presentation," Ms. Felix says, "you will all be writing your very first line of code."

Already? I turn to look at Umberto and mouth him a desperate "Help!"

Ms. Felix goes to the next slide, which looks like a chart of the alphabet with a bunch of numbers next to each letter. The weird thing is, the only numbers are ones and zeros. I know I'm not the best reader, but this CAN'T be right.

"This is binary code," Ms. Felix announces. "It's essentially the ABCs for computers. As you probably noticed, the only numbers used in binary are zeros and ones. The sequence in which they appear dictates a certain function; in this case, they represent a letter of the alphabet."

00101110001100111
10100101101010101
00110101101010101
10101010101010101
00101010101010101
10101010101010101

binary

1 2 3 4 5 6 7 8 9 10
11 12 13 14 15 16 17 18 19 20

sequence

dictates

BINARY ALPHABET			
a	1100001	A	1000001
b	1100010	B	1000010
c	1100011	C	1000011
d	1100100	D	1000100
e	1100101	E	1000101
f	1100110	F	1000110
g	1100111	G	1000111
h	1101000	H	1001000
i	1101001	I	1001001
j	1101010	J	1001010
k	1101011	K	1001011
l	1101100	L	1001100
m	1101101	M	1001101
n	1101110	N	1001110
o	1101111	O	1001111
p	1110000	P	1010000
q	1110001	Q	1010001
r	1110010	R	1010010
s	1110011	S	1010011
t	1110100	T	1010100
u	1110101	U	1010101
v	1110110	V	1010110
w	1110111	W	1010111
x	1111000	X	1011000
y	1111001	Y	1011001
z	1111010	Z	1011010

I start planning how to tell Mom
and Dad I'll be transferring into the

comedy class with Matt. There's NO WAY I'll be able to memorize all these sequences.

Ms. Felix picks up a marker and begins to write a long string of zeros and ones. "This is what my name looks like in binary," she says when she's finished. "Now, you try—with your own names, not mine."

It takes me longer than everyone else, but I plug all the smaller chunks of code together. D-e-r-e-k in binary looks like this:

1000100 - 1100101 - 1110010 - 1100101 – 1101011

Pretty cool if you're a spy; I'm not quite sure how I'll ever use this skill.

"So here's your assignment for next week," Ms. Felix says.

There's a collective groan from the class.

collective

"There HAS to be homework—there's too much material to cover in just a few months otherwise." Ms. Felix calls me up to grab a stack of handouts and pass them out. "You're going to build on the block programming—pun intended—by practicing with some online tutorials." She then tells us to check out code.org and the-cs.org. "They are nonprofit organizations committed to bringing coding into schools, especially for girls and underrepresented populations."

nonprofit

WOMEN 16%

underrepresented

On our way out, I have to bite my tongue not to ask Ms. Felix what's on the menu for tomorrow's lunch. Instead, I introduce myself to the girl who was sitting next to me.

"By the way, I'm Derek."

"I know." She points to my open

notebook page with my name in binary. "I'm Jade," she answers.

She heads to the door and the conversation ends. I run to catch up to Umberto at his locker.

"I didn't think it was possible to like the lunch servers any more than I already did." He grins. "I can't believe Ms. Felix knows so much about coding!"

I tell Umberto to calm down; Ms. Felix probably has a boyfriend.

Umberto rolls his eyes and continues. "I use those websites all the time. They're really good and also they're free."

"I'm not going to be able to access ANY website on my new laptop— my parents got me one without a wireless card."

Umberto laughs. "Old-school,

upgrade

huh? Looks like you're going to have to upgrade, my friend."

Hopefully my parents will buy the argument that I need a wireless card to complete my assignments. But Umberto's enthusiasm makes me realize it's been a while since I've been passionate about something. Skateboarding, gaming, cartooning are all things it took time to get good at; I haven't thrown myself into something new for some time. I'm not sure I'll feel that way about computer science, but I guess my parents are right—the only way to find out is to try.

I just hope the subject matter isn't completely over my head—like so many other things are.

TIME TO GET TO WORK

THANKFULLY MY PARENTS DON'T protest about getting an "I need it for school" wireless card. Dad takes me to the nearest electronics store, where we ask the clerk for one that fits inside my computer. The woman takes the plastic-enclosed card from the rack behind her.

electronics

"You want me to pop that in for you?" she asks.

I answer yes at the same instant my dad answers no.

"She knows what she's doing—we don't." I lower my voice. "It will probably take her two seconds!"

"Then you'll never learn how to maintain your own computer." Dad slaps his credit card on the counter, and the woman rings us up.

As she hands me the bag, the woman gives a little shrug that tells me she agrees with me, but Dad's the one who's paying.

Back home, we google the steps of how to install a wireless card: Take out the laptop battery then the back cover, locate the slot, insert the card, configure the new software. When we turn the power back on and the home network appears, I do feel a TINY bit proud of my accomplishment.

configure

I thank Dad for his help, then run upstairs with my provisions.

provisions

Laptop—check.

Power bars—check.

Lemonade—check.

Homework playlist cued up—check.

Bodi by my feet—check.

After running through my list several times, even a professional procrastinator like me has to get to work. I take one last second to text my friends a bunch of "going off grid" and "it's not you, it's me" memes to make sure I'm not distracted. If I'm going to have a snowball's chance at grasping this coding thing, I need to give it my undivided attention.

I'm listening.

undivided

The first tutorial on the code.org website has me creating a basic program for Angry Birds. It's a game

grunting

banished

embark

avatar

I used to play on our TV all the time until the grunting of the pigs drove Bodi so insane that Mom and Dad banished me from playing it in the family room.

Kids like Umberto, who've been programming for years, actually WRITE code, but for today's homework, we're starting off using the block method, which literally looks like the Legos I played with as a kid. The commands are different shapes and colors and snap into place like building blocks. For a visual learner like me, it's an easy way to embark on a new instructional voyage.

I drag and drop the command blocks—move forward, turn left, turn right—then hit run. After a few false starts, my bird avatar finally bounces through the maze and explodes the pig. The familiar laughing sounds on-screen let me know I've succeeded in creating my first computer program.

Nailed it!

My initial instinct is to show off to my parents but I realize learning a new skill like coding isn't a sprint—it's a marathon. I'm going to need all the endurance I can summon, so I ingest two energy bars and move on to the next tutorial.

endurance

ingest

By the time Dad sticks his head into my room to tell me to get ready for bed, I've mastered every last Angry Bird assignment, including one where the bird has to maneuver through a labyrinth of crates filled with dynamite. That time—even with all the turns—I got to the pig on the first try. I hit

mastered

dynamite

run so Dad and I can watch the game together.

"I knew you'd take to this quickly," Dad says. "Programming that laptop is going to be a breeze."

reversal

It's a real role reversal for me to be the one pumping the brakes, not Dad. "I've got a long way to go until I know what I'm doing," I say. "It's still so new."

"Small, consistent steps—that's the key to success." He tousles my hair and tells me to go brush my teeth.

associated

It's been a long time since the word *success* was associated with work coming from me. I thank Dad for the compliment, find my pajamas in the pile of clothes on the floor, and go to bed.

A HINT OF TROUBLE

AS MY GRAMMY WOULD SAY, I'VE got a "spring in my step" when I push through the front door of school the next morning. Not falling behind the pack—for once—gives me such a boost in confidence that I actually volunteer to answer a question in language arts class. Even though my answer is wrong—who knew *The*

dystopian

deterred

ambition

Giver was a dystopian novel?—I'm not deterred and answer questions in other classes too. I feel the way a student like Carly must feel every day.

At lunch, it's weird to see Ms. Felix dishing out Salisbury steak and mashed potatoes knowing she's so good at computer science. When I mention it to Carly, she just shrugs.

"Maybe working in the cafeteria is fun," she says. "Maybe she wanted more flexible hours. Ambition isn't the only factor when choosing a career."

I reach across the table and gently knock on Carly's forehead. "Hello! What alien creature has taken over Carly Rodriquez's brain?"

Carly smiles. "I guess that didn't sound much like me."

"You're the most ambitious person I know. You used to finger paint to-do lists in kindergarten! I barely knew my alphabet back then."

kindergarten

I don't just make Carly laugh; I actually get her to shoot chocolate milk out her nose, which I take as a huge comedy victory. She hurries to wipe herself off. "You made me ruin this shirt!" she says. "Chocolate never comes out!"

chocolate

"What are you talking about? I've gotten chocolate on every piece of clothing I've ever worn. Just wash it when you get home." So much for having an audience that appreciates good comedic timing.

Carly continues to fixate on the stain, which is hardly noticeable. "I can't walk around like this all day. People will think I'm a slob!"

noticeable

It dawns on me that Carly isn't going to shrug this off, so instead of telling her she's wrong, I change tactics and try to calm her down. Without realizing it, I use the same soothing voice my mother uses with her canine patients.

"It's fine," I tell Carly. "No one but you knows it's there."

She throws down her sandwich, still fussing with her shirt.

"Hey—you seem really tense. Is everything okay?"

Carly then does something I'm completely unprepared for. She starts crying. I nearly jump across the table just to get her to stop. "Everything's going to be fine! It's no big deal!"

"I feel so awful," Carly says between sobs. "I'm such a loser."

How is this possible? Carly is the most accomplished kid I know. "Carly, if you're a loser, what does

tense

accomplished

that make me? The most monumental idiot in the history of the world?"

She doesn't even crack a smile, just wipes her cheek with the back of her hand. "I'm sorry," she says. "I'm sure the last thing you want to do during your valuable free time is to get me to stop crying."

Even though she's 100 percent correct, I pat her on the back and tell her that's what friends are for.

"I don't know what's wrong with me lately." She brushes the crumbs off the table as if they're contaminated.

A nagging thought bubbles up from deep inside me—this isn't *girl* stuff Carly's going through, is it? That embarrassing puberty material we learned about in health class? If it is, I'll have to fake-choke on my

puberty

mashed potatoes and get out of here. PRONTO.

I'm eternally grateful when Umberto slides up to the table and tells us how Dave in his science class bought a box of crickets from the pet store, then let them loose in the ceiling tiles above Ms. Miller's desk. Umberto acts out the chirping and classroom chaos with so much energy that he cheers up Carly in two seconds flat. Which means I don't have to pretend to choke on my lunch—also a good thing.

Thinking about that puberty junk from health class makes me wonder if I'm going to start acting weird soon too. I can't speak for Carly but I'm not sure if I can handle life getting any more complicated than it already is.

crickets

WHO DIS?

I'M WALKING BODI BEFORE DINNER when a text pops up with a number I've never seen before. I'm curious where the link inside the text bubble will lead but I know enough about the negative side of technology to realize I shouldn't click on a link if I don't know where it originated. I tuck the phone back into my pocket and lead Bodi toward the dog park.

originated

gusto

Letting Bodi off-leash in the fenced-in park is one of my favorite parts of the day. Even though he's older, he still chases squirrels with the gusto of a pup. I drape Bodi's leash on the chain-link fence, lean back, and watch my dog run with abandon.

A series of *dings* go off in my pocket. Five more texts with links. I finally give in and type out a response communicating that I don't know who this is.

One second later, I receive a selfie from Jade—the girl from coding class. I ask her how she got my cell number since I don't remember giving it to her.

She texts back that finding someone's number takes two seconds.

WHAT? Is this new girl a hacker?

JUST CLICK THE LINK, she texts back.

After a few moments of internal debate, I take my chances and click.

Up pops a video that looks like it was shot on a webcam in what I'm guessing is Jade's room. The view is of her laptop and an incredibly fast-paced video game involving a group of pirate kittens using daggers and swords in what appears to be a feline mutiny. The action and graphics remind me of when Matt and I tested the game Arctic Ninja a while ago. There is absolutely no way Jade wrote the code for this new game!

I check to see if Bodi's okay, then furiously text Jade back. *Of course I coded it*, she responds. *You think*

daggers

mutiny

I'd waste my time playing a game someone else created?

I keep the fact that I've proudly wasted tons of time playing games other people created to myself.

Compared to Jade's game, the work I did on Angry Birds yesterday feels amateur at best. My fear of being over my head in this class has totally come true. Why did she have to show off like that? And how exactly did she get my cell number?

I whistle for Bodi, then fasten the leash to his collar. In a second, this went from being the best part of my day to the worst.

Thanks, Jade.

amateur

WHAT IS THAT?

THE LAST THING I EVER WANT TO do on a Friday night is homework, but Jade has me terrified so I strap in for another long night. First, I stop into Mom's office to let her know I'll be working through dinner. I make sure to sound extra dedicated in the hopes that she'll give me what I REALLY want—dinner in my room on that little bed tray she uses

bed tray

whenever one of us is sick. (No self-respecting coder ever got called downstairs by his mother for dinner.)

As the kid of a veterinarian, I know to drop Bodi off in the house before heading into Mom's office. Bodi's a docile dog, but the last thing Mom wants is an animal showdown in her waiting room. It's always fun to walk into her office; I've seen everything from cats wearing diapers to people who insist on lining their dog crate with family photos so their pet won't be lonely while they board. But I'm flabbergasted when I walk into the waiting room after hours today and see the tiniest horse I've ever seen.

"I've seen Great Danes bigger than that pony!" I tell my mother.

docile

showdown

Mom smiles. "It's not a pony—it's a miniature horse. Her name is Maggie."

"She's not even three feet tall!" I've been around animals my whole life, but it feels totally weird to be taller than a HORSE.

I'm extra gentle when I stroke Maggie's mane, using the same soothing voice I use when meeting any new animal. I ask Mom why Maggie's here.

"Remember how Frank was trained to be a service animal?" she begins.

How could I possibly forget about Frank? He was a capuchin but I always thought of him as a tiny, furry brother. He lived with us until my YouTube antics made the organization we got him from revoke our

revoke

status as his foster family. Thinking about Frank warms me up inside; remembering my screwup makes me cringe.

"Well, Maggie's also a service animal," Mom continues. "She's part of an organization in Calabasas that takes miniature horses into the community for therapy."

therapy

"Don't they get squished when people ride them?"

Mom shakes her head and laughs. "You don't *ride* a miniature horse. The staff take them to visit patients at the children's hospital or assisted-living facilities. Because they're loving by nature, they make great one-on-one companions for trauma victims."

backtrack

I backtrack to make sure I understand what she's saying. "So there's a charity that takes miniature horses to visit people who are sick or sad?"

"Exactly. Maggie just got back from visiting a school in Northridge that got damaged by an earthquake."

A plan begins to form in my feeble mind. Maggie just might be the solution I've been looking for.

solution

"How long is Maggie going to be here?" I ask.

Mom glances at the clock. "Maybe another hour."

I tell her I'll be right back.

If there's one person who needs a pick-me-up from a pint-sized horse, it's Carly.

I'VE CREATED A
MONSTER

lovefest

THE SQUEAL OF DELIGHT THAT comes out of Carly when she sees Maggie almost sends the poor horse galloping out of the office. Carly realizes her mistake, lowers her voice, and approaches the miniature horse slowly. As soon as Maggie finally lays eyes on Carly, the lovefest is mutual. Maggie gets up on her hind legs, leans in toward Carly, and nuzzles.

"She's hugging me." Carly's voice is barely a whisper but I can tell she's about to explode. "A baby horse is hugging me!"

Mom explains that Maggie is actually not a baby but a full-grown adult horse. "You're right about one thing, Carly—that is definitely a hug!"

extensive

I hope Mom doesn't have to perform an extensive exam on Maggie because I'm not sure she'll be able to tear Carly away.

I try to guide Carly and Maggie toward the waiting room seats where they'd be more comfortable but neither of them will move. I know this is a massive detour from focusing on my coding assignment but helping a friend in need is a bigger priority. Carly really needs this.

Mom talks us through the exam she's giving Maggie—weighing her, checking her teeth, recording her heartbeat. She puts on her reading glasses and checks out Maggie's front right hoof. "She's got a hairline fracture here. She might need to see a farrier."

farrier

I explain to Carly that a farrier is someone who specializes in horse hooves. It only happens once in a blue moon, so I never miss the opportunity to teach something new to Carly instead of the other way around.

Mom has always loved Carly and it's nice to see them bonding throughout Maggie's examination. I didn't say anything to Mom about how Carly's been acting lately but it almost seems as if she can tell that Carly needs some extra TLC.

"How about if I talk to Nancy at the equine-therapy organization?" Mom suggests. "Maybe see if you can spend more time with Maggie."

equine

Carly smiles as if she just won a lottery worth ten billion dollars.

"Would you mind keeping Maggie company while I make a few notes in her chart?" Mom gives me a wink as she leaves the room. I always knew moms had superpowers with their OWN kids, but mine seems to know what other kids need too. Maybe being a vet enhances her empathy for ALL creatures.

enhances

empathy

"This mini horse is too cute for words." Carly snaps several selfies with Maggie. "My phone is going

batty

entrenched

to run out of memory with all the photos I'm taking."

I'm not as batty over the miniature horse as Carly is, but it IS pretty funny petting a horse the size of a Labrador retriever.

"Can you imagine if we took Maggie to school?" Carly asks. "Kids would go nuts!"

"She DOES go to schools," I respond. "I guess we could ask." As soon as the words leave my mouth and I see Carly's eyes light up, I realize I've made a giant mistake. This idea is now permanently entrenched in Carly's brain.

Let's just hope my mom can pull enough strings to make this happen.

DAD TO THE RESCUE

BY THE TIME CARLY LEAVES, IT'S nearly six o'clock and Dad is putting the finishing touches on the chicken Caesar salad he made for dinner.

"Mom says it's okay to start without her since she's still working. What do you say we make this a living room picnic and throw on some old *Looney Tunes*?"

classic

commonplace

I tell him I'd love to watch classic cartoons, but I've put off my coding homework for long enough. "I should take this plate to go."

Dad nods and serves some salad onto a plate. "One chicken Caesar for the road."

I thank him and run up to my room to begin a night in front of the computer screen.

The assignment is to write a "computer program" for completing a commonplace, everyday task—like making a PB&J or tying your shoes. I flip open my laptop, crack my knuckles like all the hackers do in the movies...and that's as far as I get before texting Umberto for help.

When he doesn't respond, I try calling but get his voice mail. "I'm in over my head," I say after the beep.

"All I've ever coded before are those simple Angry Birds block patterns and writing my name in binary. This JavaScript format doesn't make any sense. Call me back!"

format

As soon as I set down my phone, I hear two tiny taps on the side of my door. "Knock, knock," Dad says. "Homework trouble?"

Instead of answering, I launch myself facedown onto my bed and let my legs hang over the edge.

Dad walks to my desk and picks up my assignment sheet. "Okay, so step one is to pick an everyday task. That shouldn't be too hard. What's something you do every day?"

"Yearn to be in comedy class," I mumble into my comforter.

yearn

"Right now you look like you're ready for bed, so why don't you write code for that?"

I grunt into my pillow but Dad pulls me by the feet until I get up.

"So what are the steps in getting ready for bed?"

"Brushing my teeth?" I sit up and see Dad's gaze shift the way it does when he's got an idea. He sets down my assignment sheet and opens one of my sketchbooks.

"If I were animating Derek getting ready for bed, I would start with a storyboard." His pencil moves across the page making the familiar rectangular panels he does every day for work. He hands me the book full of panels ready to be filled.

"First, I take a shower." I draw a stick-figure version of me under running water. "Then I put on my pajamas."

My pencil moves to the next box

and I start to smile. Drawing has always been the easiest way for me to understand every subject in school—why would coding be any different? By changing how I think about approaching coding assignments, maybe I won't find them to be such an enigma. Nice job, Dad.

enigma

He pats me on the shoulder and leaves me to my work. Not long after, I have six completed story-board panels:

TAKE SHOWER	WASH HAIR	DRY OFF
PUT ON PAJAMAS	BRUSH TEETH	PRETEND TO FLOSS

All I have to do now is follow the example on the assignment sheet and translate my drawings into code. THAT'S the tricky part.

I focus on the first drawing of stick-figure Derek in the shower and try to remember when Ms. Felix had us write our names in binary. I take my time and copy the sequence of commands and punctuation marks that translates my commands into the language of a computer program. Then I go back and swap out the pieces from the sample task with the steps of getting ready for bed.

It takes every ounce of willpower not to rush, but I'm glad when I double-check the assignment sheet and find a line in the instructions

I had missed: *MAKE SURE TO INCLUDE EVERY NECESSARY STEP. SKIPPING OVER JUST ONE COMMAND WILL RENDER YOUR CODE INOPERABLE.*

inoperable

I look over my six little Dereks in their story panels and the heavy feeling that my work is far from over starts to sink in. You can't brush your teeth without grabbing some toothpaste and showers don't just turn on by themselves. It kills me to have to go back and add in the additional steps, but the last thing I need is another graded assignment handed back to me with *See me* written at the top.

After what seems like an eternity, I finally hit save and I can't believe my eyes:

```
// A program to get ready for
bed.
    var self = {
        name: "Derek",
        age: "12",
        job: "student"};
    var house = {
        address: "123 Internet
Street"};
function getReadyForBed(){
    // Use the Bathroom
    self.walkToBathroom();
    house.turnOnWater("warm",
"bathroom");
    self.takeShower();
    house.turnOffWater("bathroom");
    self.dry("towel");
    self.dressUpperBody("pajamas");
    self.dressLowerBody("pajamas");
    self.brushTeeth("120 seconds");
    self.floss();
```

```
    // Take Care of Bodi
    self.goDownstairs();
    house.turnOnLight("kitchen");
    house.turnOnWater("cool",
"kitchen");
    self.fillBowl("water");
    house.turnOffWater("kitchen");
    self.placeBowl("floor");
    house.turnOffLight("kitchen");
    self.goUpstairs();
    // Wrap Up
    self.greet(self.mom, self.dad);
    self.walkTo("bedroom");
    house.plugInPhone();
    self. setAlarm("6:30 a.m.");
    self.sleep();
}
getReadyForBed();
```

It took a lot longer than I
wanted, but I did it—I wrote my

first computer program without the help of a tutorial! My huge grin is interrupted by an even bigger yawn, and I decide it's time to follow my own instructions and hit the hay.

I spend the rest of the weekend recovering from all the work with lots of YouTube. When I get to school on Monday, Umberto grabs me before I get to my locker.

"I'm sorry I never got back to you this weekend." He pants as he catches his breath. "I got my phone taken away at the dinner table on Friday. Matt kept sending me videos of his routine and that made me laugh while my grandmother was telling us about her hip surgery."

I tell him it's okay and fill him in

on Dad's brilliant strategy to use drawing as a way to visualize coding. "Wait until you see what I did!" I dig into my backpack to show him the printout of my program, but the paper slips from my hands and slides across the hall.

retrieve

I rush to retrieve it, but two black combat boots get to it first.

"Hi, Jade!" Umberto says.

I glare at him, but I'm also curious what the class genius will say about my program.

She looks it over and hands it back. "This yours?"

"Yeah." I reach out to take it, still unable to read her reaction.

"Weird. I don't know anyone who takes a shower with his clothes on."

I guess I didn't translate my drawings into code as well as I thought I did.

Jade drops the paper into my hands and walks off without another word, taking my self-esteem with her.

MS. FELIX SERVES UP SOME CODING

IT'S NOT EVEN LUNCHTIME YET and Carly's asked me a dozen times when she can see Maggie again. I begin to wonder if calling her over to meet the mini horse was such a good idea. The last thing Carly needs is something else to obsess over—not to mention we're all pretty sick of feigning excitement whenever

> I don't feel very well today.

feigning

pipsqueak

Carly shows us another picture of Maggie on her phone.

"If I hear one more comment about that pipsqueak pony, I'm going to puke," Matt says.

"You're just mad I called Carly instead of you," I reply.

"That's not true!"

"It's a LITTLE true," I say. "I only hope Mom can talk Maggie's organization into letting Carly spend more time with the therapy horses."

Matt buries his head in his hands. "Please don't say there are MORE of them."

As we head to the cafeteria, I make a mental note to restrain my equine enthusiasm around my best friend.

When I get to the front of the food line, Ms. Felix gives me the sign with her spatula wave. "You ready for class?" she asks. "Lots of new stuff to cover today."

I nod and smile as if I am. Before I move down the counter, I linger a few seconds to see if she might scoop a few extra meatballs on my plate, but she doesn't. Claudia Jordan is behind me and nudges me to move on.

linger

I spot Umberto at our usual table and am a little discouraged to see HE got extra meatballs. Why did I think Ms. Felix would reward a slacker like me?

discouraged

When Umberto opens repl.it—the sharing platform we use in class—I'm shocked to see how many pages of coding he did. "Dude, how long did that take you?"

Umberto shrugs. "I don't know—two hours?"

His comment makes me almost choke on my meatball, and Ms. Tatreaux hurries toward me like she's about to give me the Heimlich maneuver. Luckily, I swallow before half the school can watch a kindergarten teacher save me from choking.

One of Umberto's great qualities is that he never rubs how smart he is in your face. Instead of gloating about his coding skills, he changes the subject and asks me if I noticed Ms. McCoddle's new tattoo. She got a rose on her wrist last year and just added a new one of an orchid on her other arm.

gloating

orchid

"If she keeps adding flowers, we're going to have to start watering her," Umberto adds.

I nod as if I'm listening but all I

can think about is how my coding assignment is so much lamer than Umberto's. And according to Jade, my program calls for a fully clothed shower. I don't even want to THINK about the perfect lines of code SHE came up with.

Why did I ever let my parents convince me to take this impossibly hard elective?! Matt may be the one in comedy class, but the joke's on me.

LESS FUN BY THE MINUTE

coerced

MY RANTS MUST BE GETTING ON Umberto's nerves because as we head down the hall after school, he stops in his tracks and almost shouts, "Derek, you VOLUNTEERED to take this class; no one coerced you to learn something new."

I beg to differ, but I know that arguing with him won't make things better. The first thing I see as we enter coding class is a crowd of kids surrounding Jade's desk.

"Pirate Kittens is more fun than Candy Crush!" Maria says. "I can't believe someone I know made such an awesome game."

"It's so fast," Taylor adds. "And the graphics are incredible."

Has Jade always gone to this school or did she transfer into this class just to make me look bad? I sneak a peek over Maria's shoulder in time to see Jade navigate to her dashboard and hit share.

"Now you guys can play Pirate Kittens whenever you want," Jade says. "Knock yourselves out."

The horde of eager gamers race to their phones to enjoy the game.

horde

"I'm too busy to play any new games," I tell Jade. "You don't have to share it with me."

"Don't worry, I didn't." She doesn't even look up.

"Good afternoon!" Ms. Felix bounces into the room as if she hadn't already worked a full day. I wish I had some of that energy right about now.

What's Jade's problem, anyway?

Ms. Felix asks us if we watched the tutorials and did the assignments. She's thrilled when every hand goes up.

"Before you took this class, how many of you used to watch coding tutorials on YouTube?"

Almost half the class raises their hands. I had no idea so many kids watched YouTube to LEARN things.

"How many of you already know JavaScript?" she continues.

The number of raised hands decreases but Umberto, Taylor, and Jade continue to hold theirs up.

decreases

"Anyone know Python? Or HTML?"

The only hand left up belongs to Jade.

Ms. Felix digs around in her giant purse and pulls out her phone. "It used to take a whole room to harness the computing power you kids now carry around in your pockets."

This isn't going to be one of those "In my day" speeches, is it?

Ms. Felix waves her phone in the air. "But these devices are also like slot machines—we check them a zillion times a day to see if we've won. Even if you get mentioned in a post or someone shoots you a text, you're still losing because you gave away your attention for free."

I'm confused—is Ms. Felix for or against technology?

"Over a billion people on the planet use smartphones—and only two companies control almost every one of them," she continues. "The reason I'm teaching this class is so you kids can have a stake in how your brains get used. I want *you* to be in control of where your minds go, not a roomful of engineers competing for your attention 24/7. Technology isn't neutral. Kids who code will be

neutral

shaping the future of the planet. THAT'S why I'm here. It's why you should be here too."

I've heard rumblings about the "attention economy," mostly when Mr. Ennis taught that YouTube class. But I've never heard anyone be so urgent in her or his views as Ms. Felix is now.

rumblings

economy

Do any of my classmates think about this stuff or am I the only one happy to just swipe and play? Are we going to learn to make games and apps in this class or what? Is it bad that I just want to animate some of my stick figures and have FUN?

urgent

Finally, Ms. Felix glances at the list of students in front of her. "Okay, Jade, why don't you share your work with us?"

rephrase

"I already did," she answers.

With everyone but me.

"Let me rephrase the question," Ms. Felix says. "Why don't you come on up here and show us what you've created?"

Jade plods her combat boots to the front of the room. "It's nothing extravagant," she sighs and pulls out her phone. "Mind if I mirror?"

Unreal. Is she going to see how she looks right now? In front of everyone?

Ms. Felix nods and Jade taps on her phone. In an instant, the home screen of Jade's phone is displayed on Ms. Felix's monitor.

Oh, THAT kind of mirror.

She takes us through the menus

of Pirate Kittens, explaining that the game is based on her own calico at home. "I named her Anne Bonny, after the famous female pirate."

calico

I look around the room. She's got everyone mesmerized—including Ms. Felix. That familiar sinking feeling that I'll never be good at anything creeps into my stomach. I'm the one who could really use a visit from Maggie right now.

Like everything else I've had to work to understand, I know if I'm going to keep up in this class, I have to buckle down. I'm usually too busy watching epic fails on YouTube to bother with tutorials that could improve my skills, but I'm not about to let this new girl code her way around the rest of us so easily. I'll stay up past midnight every night if I have to; I'm going to catch up to Jade if it kills me.

Share THAT!

JADE GOES VIRAL

THE ENTIRE SCHOOL IS CUCKOO for Pirate Kittens. The game spreads like last year's wildfire, with kids playing alone or in groups at every break. I can't even walk to class without hearing that annoying meowing background music around every corner. I'm not even playing this game and I can't get the song out of my head.

cuckoo

It turns out Pirate Kittens isn't Jade's first app; she's got a backlist of games she freely shares with anyone who asks—which is pretty much everyone but me. I think I'm the only kid here who DOESN'T play her stupid games. What'll she come up with next—a game where your avatar ransacks trash cans outside a hospital for bracelets?

ransacks

While Jade rides her popularity wave, I spend every waking moment watching coding tutorials. Over the weekend, I lock myself in my room on my still-has-no-applications laptop and attempt to write code for my OWN game.

rip-off

Is Pirate Dogs too much of a rip-off? Or Buccaneer Cats?

buccaneer

It's HARD coming up with original ideas.

And even if I do pull some fantastic concept out of my imagination, I still have to write the code that'll make the engine of that idea work. I text and call Umberto several times asking for clarification.

"I keep getting the same error message," I whine. "I feel like I'm banging my head against a wall."

"Dude, there can't be even ONE typo," Umberto explains. "If there's one mistake in the code, it won't work. You have to be super methodical when you check your work."

methodical

I'm not sure what that means, but it sounds like I have to drastically

proofreading

symbols

increase the level of proofreading that I usually do with homework. If every report or essay I handed in at school had to have ZERO mistakes, I wouldn't have gotten past preschool. I might even have to resort to running my homework by some classmates—something I've always been too embarrassed to do. I know Carly and Umberto edit each other's essays in Google Docs all the time. Collaborative homework always seemed like an unnecessary and additional step, but I might have to jump on the bandwagon.

Umberto patiently explains that you have to string together words and symbols in a specific order if you want them to make sense.

"It's the same way a sentence works in *any* language," Umberto continues. "You have to arrange the nouns, verbs, adjectives, and prepositions in a certain way—but with numbers. It's called syntax."

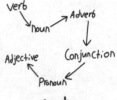

syntax

"You know I stink at grammar!" I say. "Now I'm supposed to learn the grammar of a computer?"

"It might be difficult in the beginning, but you'll catch on."

"I'm glad one of us thinks so."

"When you create something that matches the vision you had for it in your head, it's really cool," Umberto says.

I tell him that's how I feel when I finish a good drawing.

systematic

"Exactly. Plus, being so systematic with coding helps you IRL too. Having a coding mind-set lets me see the big picture in other things. I'm much better at working through all kinds of obstacles now."

obstacles

If either of my parents had said that, I'd be running to the bathroom to hurl. But Umberto's a kid; it would be dumb not to take the advice of someone who's learning the same things as I am.

"Besides, being on the Internet shouldn't be just a spectator sport—you need to create stuff too. Mr. Ennis and Ms. Felix both talked about that."

I have to admit, I've thought about Ms. Felix's technology rant often in the past few days. Maybe I SHOULD be paying more attention to where my attention is going.

"Coding can be frustrating," Umberto adds. "But stick with it—I think you'll be great."

abilities

There it is again—that vote of confidence in my abilities. Umberto's rarely wrong. Why start doubting him now?

Before we hang up, I ask him about Jade.

"That girl has some mad skills," Umberto answers. "I love Ms. Felix, but Jade could be teaching that class. She's not too bad-looking either."

Never mind what I said earlier; if Umberto has a crush on my coding-class nemesis, his judgment is totally compromised. I thank him for his help and hang up.

I'm about to get back to work when I see Bodi sitting by the bedroom door. I realize I never took him out to pee and it's after ten o'clock. Hours have passed while I was lost in my work—maybe I DO have what it takes to be a coder after all.

A DIFFICULT CHOICE

MATT'S BEEN BUGGING ME TO check out his brother's band for months. Before Jamie left for college, Matt and I would hear him practicing in his bedroom all the time, only it sounded less like music and more like an angry rooster. When Matt would ask me what I thought, I'd just smile and give him a thumbs-up. There's no polite way to tell your best friend that his brother's music stinks.

But I guess all those years of practice paid off because Jamie's band has quite a following now; they have over three thousand likes on their Facebook page. The name of his band is Velvet Incinerator, which doesn't really make sense until Jamie explained that the whole point of a band's name is that it DOESN'T make sense.

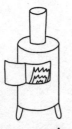

incinerator

amoeba

Velvet Incinerator usually plays at bars and clubs up and down the coast. Tonight, however, they're doing an all-ages show at Amoeba Records, so Matt and I can finally see Jamie play. To make sure there's a big crowd, we spent the weekend helping Jamie put up flyers outside every local coffee shop. Matt invited half of our school too.

When I asked Carly what time she wanted to meet us at the show, she said she "wasn't up for it." Carly's usually up for anything so something must be really bothering her. Plus, she dropped out of the after-school drawing class and Carly never drops out of ANYTHING.

Matt's too excited about going to Amoeba to share my concern. "We can head in early with Jamie and look at all the movies and music while he sets up," Matt says. "Last time I was there, they had a whole new section of Funko Pops!"

"We'll see if we can beat our previous record," I add. Whenever Matt and I go to a store together, we keep a tally of how quickly someone comes over and tells us to be quiet. Our current time to beat is a mere twenty-eight seconds. If they gave out Olympic medals for in-store antics, Matt and I would bring home the gold every time.

It's pretty rare to have the same favorite store as one of your parents, but Dad loves Amoeba Records as much as I do. He always comes up with an excuse to be "in the neighborhood" so he can get lost in all the cool stuff there is to see. When he found out last week that's where Jamie's show was, he immediately volunteered to drive us home. I've got a sneaking suspicion he'll show up early to browse through the bins of cult records pretending he's there to see Jamie's band.

My thoughts are pulled back to

cult

school when I turn a corner outside the administration wing and almost trip over someone. I never even knew Jade existed until coding class, but now I bump into her all the time. She barely looks up but surprises me with a quick nod, which is an improvement from our last few interactions.

administration

I don't know why Jade keeps to herself so much. She's a coding rock star and could easily be friends with anyone, but I don't think I've ever seen her in a conversation with another classmate. Her best friend seems to be her phone—which makes me think yet again about what Ms. Felix said. But I don't want to get sucked into the rabbit hole of the am-I-a-slave-to-my-phone argument, so I keep on walking.

I'm hit with another surprise when I run into Carly slipping out of Ms. Costa's office. Ms. Costa is the guidance counselor who's been at our school the longest; she's an expert in helping kids with serious issues. After Taylor's dad died last year, she supported him in dealing with his grief.

grief

"Oh!" Carly says. "What are you doing here?"

I tell her Ms. McCoddle asked me to drop something off to the vice principal on my way to science. "What are YOU doing here?"

nimble

I can see the wheels turning inside Carly's nimble mind. Should she make up an excuse or tell me the truth? In the end, she shrugs and admits she had a meeting with Ms. Costa.

The moron in me wants to bust Carly's chops but an even bigger part of me can see she's troubled, and joking around isn't the correct response. Judging by Carly's expression right now, a teeny-tiny horse might not be the answer either.

expression

"Was Ms. Costa helpful?" It sounds like the kind of question my mom would ask and I pray it doesn't make things worse.

"She was," Carly answers slowly. "It made me feel better to know lots of kids feel anxious sometimes too."

"You know what else helps people feel better?" I ask. "Doing something fun. Come with us to hear Jamie's band!"

Carly declines again.

"Aww, come on," I say. "You just want to watch me beg."

A smile slowly crosses her face. Finally!

"I don't want you to beg," she says. "I just don't feel like being around a bunch of people right now. I think I'll stay home and binge-watch some old Nickelodeon shows."

Normally I'm always up for vegging out in front of the TV, but we're talking about seeing a concert by a band we actually know at one of the coolest places in L.A. I implore Carly to join us one more time.

implore

"I'm FINE!" Carly says. "Stop worrying."

Carly's tone tells me I may have pushed too hard. I hurry to change the subject.

"My mom left a message at the equine-therapy place," I say.

"Maybe we can see the horses next weekend."

"That sounds great." Carly rests her hand on my arm. "Thanks for being such a good friend."

We go our separate ways but Carly's words echo inside me for the rest of the afternoon. What WOULD a good friend do in this situation? The truth is, I know the answer. But it's not going to be easy for another one of my friends.

At the end of the day, I catch up with Matt at his locker. "Something came up. I won't be able to go tonight."

"WHAT?!" Matt shouts. "We've been planning this for weeks!"

"I know ... there's just something I have to do."

"It better be something important

incurable

like discovering the antidote to an incurable disease," Matt says.

"It IS that important," I answer. "I wouldn't be bailing on you if it wasn't."

Intentionally disappointing a best friend is something I try to avoid at all costs. No matter how much of a good time I'd have with Matt tonight, thinking about Carly home alone watching old TV shows would suck all the fun out of it. Matt wants me to see his brother's band, but Carly needs a friend even more.

Matt shakes his head. "Guess I'll have to go to my first real rock show alone."

"I can go!" Umberto skids to a halt in front of us. "I didn't think I could get a ride, but I can."

Now that Umberto's in, I wonder if my Good Samaritan routine is overkill and I should be celebrating Jamie's new CD with my friends. My brain fart is temporary, however, and I text Carly to ask if I can hang out at her house tonight.

overkill

Suppose she says no? Shouldn't I have asked her before I pulled the rug out from Matt? Thankfully, Carly texts back *YES!*

I tell Matt and Umberto to have fun and run to catch Carly at the bus stop.

"I know how much you wanted to go to the concert," she says. "You really don't have to keep me company—I'm GOOD."

I know she's giving me an out, but I don't take it.

"Who could pass on an *iCarly* marathon with the ORIGINAL Carly?"

I respond. "Miniature horses couldn't keep me away."

The huge grin on Carly's face as we wait for the bus tells me I made the right decision.

THE BUDDY SYSTEM

MATT AND UMBERTO TEXT ME A dozen pics of how much fun they're having at Jamie's CD release party, but spending the night reciting catchphrases from old TV shows is fun too. After we finish binging, Carly pulls out her laptop. She logs in to the school's website to check the grades on our last test and is disappointed they haven't been

reciting

posted yet. (I, on the other hand, am elated.) She opens another tab to check out next week's lunch menu.

"That's so weird..." Carly's forehead wrinkles. "My mom just put money in my account yesterday. Why does it say I'm at zero?"

"Did you buy pizza for Ms. McCoddle's entire class and not invite me?" I ask.

She ignores my joke and hits refresh several times. The account is still empty...and her frown is back.

refresh

"The page is probably just down for maintenance," I suggest. "This sort of thing happens on the meme site all the time. Let me check mine. I'm sure it's a temporary glitch."

glitch

Carly turns her laptop toward me

and I log in. When the page loads, my lunch balance also shows up at zero dollars.

"See, I told you. It'll be back to normal by morning."

"I hope so." Carly still looks worried. Thankfully, the number of unopened emails in my inbox steals her focus. "OMG, Derek. When was the last time you checked your email?"

"Uhm...last month?"

I need to be constantly reminded to check my mailbox on the school's network. It's a good thing Carly points it out, because there's an email from Ms. Felix announcing she's partnering the class for the next assignment.

constantly

"NEXT assignment?" I say. "I haven't even finished the last one."

I practically throw myself across the room. "I'm doomed!"

"It's not that bad." Carly points to the screen. "At least you're paired with someone who knows how to code."

"Umberto?" I pop up.

"Not exactly."

I slowly drag myself back to Carly's computer to face the music head-on. Sure enough, I'm partnered with Jade.

"That's good, right?" Carly asks. "She's seems knowledgeable. You'll probably learn a lot."

knowledgeable

I pretend to bang my head against Carly's desk. Spending time with Jade is not my idea of fun. Even worse, Jade is probably thinking the same about me.

When Tuesday morning rolls around, I haven't even finished

entering the combination to my locker before Jade taps me on the shoulder. "I'll be at your house at three o'clock to get cracking on the new app assignment," she says. "Should take twenty minutes but I'm budgeting ten times that since I'm working with you."

"My thoughts exactly."

"So you agree the deadweight variable in this equation is you?" Jade cracks the first smile I've ever seen. "See you at three."

variable

We haven't started working together yet and I'm already praying for this week to be over.

"You don't know where I live," I call after her.

"Of course I do," she says. "Took me less than thirty seconds to find out."

Umberto may be right about

Jade's mad skills, but right now she's making me plain old MAD.

At three o'clock on the dot Jade appears at the door. Her laptop is attached to her back with some kind of elaborate strap system.

"Are you going skydiving?" I ask. "Because it looks like you—"

skydiving

"Brought a parachute? Yeah, I get it." She plops into a chair at the kitchen table and stares at me with an expression that says, "Well?"

parachute

I open my laptop and take the chair beside her. Before I can offer her a drink or a snack—as my parents have reinforced a thousand times—she pulls out a bag of pistachios and an old-fashioned plaid thermos. She doesn't ask me if I want any, which is fine because I DON'T.

reinforced

pistachios

"First things first," Jade says. "Do you want to learn this or do you just want to get the assignment done as quickly as possible?"

It's a ridiculous question. Who DOESN'T want to be finished with homework in the fastest amount of time? But because I want to torment her, I tell her the exact opposite—that I can't wait to learn from her vast experience. In reality I want to spend the absolute minimum amount of time with Jade, but I'm willing to sacrifice my own wishes to make her even more miserable than I am. However, she seems unfazed by my answer; instead, she pops another pistachio into her mouth and begins typing.

HOMEWORK ON WEEKENDS

unfazed

"Based on your current coding abilities, I think we should start with something pretty generic. How does a homework-organization app sound?"

"Like something I'd never down-load in a million years," I answer.

She keeps her eyes on the screen and gives the faintest hint of a nod. "It might be unpopular, but it's perfect to practice coding."

I take a deep breath to stop myself from saying something snotty and pull up a chair beside her.

Surprisingly, Jade takes the time to explain every line of code she types. "Okay, what's wrong with this?" she asks.

```
public boolean
getAssignmentStatus(){
    return isSubmitted;
}
```

generic

I give her command a quick scan. "Seems fine to me."

She shakes her head and tells me to look closer.

This time I don't just pretend to look. I stare at each and every letter like a detective searching a crime scene.

"I think it's missing a word?"

"Are you asking me or telling me?" Jade tilts her head.

"I'm TELLING you."

Jade fixes the error on her screen.

```
public boolean
getAssignmentStatus(){
    return self.isSubmitted;
}
```

"Good. That's how thorough you need to be from here on in." Jade

consistent

Sir Isaac Newton discovered gravity.

concise

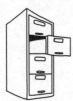

repository

data

goes on about how important it is to be consistent and concise in your work. "You should back up everything to GitHub; it's like a repository for code. And you'll want to keep a program log too, otherwise you'll never learn from your mistakes."

I keep my mouth shut and don't tell her I hardly ever learn from my mistakes, although she's probably figured that out already.

She points to my monitor. "Your battery's down to six percent. You don't want to lose any data."

Jade is actually being helpful, I think as I run upstairs to get my power cord. Maybe there was a method to Ms. Felix's madness when she paired us up after all.

When I come back down, Jade hands me my phone and tells me I got a text from Matt.

"You read my texts?!"

"No," she replies with a massive eye roll. "But the ding interrupted my flow. You'll have to shut off notifications if you want to *really* get down to business."

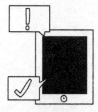

notifications

I look at Jade's desktop; she's got a dozen open screens she's working on at the same time.

"My dad helped me write a program that stops videos on YouTube from going straight to autoplay," she says. "I wrote another one that blocks all the ads, which make the videos load slowly." She shivers as if shaking off an itchy thought.

"I'm not sure I understand

how this app works yet. Isn't the assignment to write an app that we can use in everyday life?"

Jade talks slowly and calmly as if I'm a two-year-old. "It's a scheduling app that helps you organize your homework."

"What's there to organize? You open a book, you do the problems. Done." I try convincing Jade that we should write a quiz app instead. "Like on Sporcle," I say. "I got a hundred percent on the trivia quizzes for *Arrow* and the *Flash*."

"You must be so proud," Jade says from behind her screen.

"Don't you have any hobbies other than coding?" I ask. "What's your favorite show?"

"I don't watch TV."

I dig for more details. "Not on your phone? Not on an iPad?" *Not in the living room with your dog?*

"Nope." Jade then points to my laptop and we get back to work.

We continue for the next hour with Jade shuffling between explaining things and barking out commands. At five o'clock, she abruptly tells me she has to go.

I stare at the screen in front of me. "I wrote six pages of code!"

"Next time you'll write twelve," Jade says. "It's my own version of Moore's law."

"I have no idea who this Moore person is; all I know is this is MORE work than I've ever done in one sitting."

Jade doesn't laugh, just straps on her laptop and heads out. I'm not sure whether I should feel impressed or completely dissed.

This girl is half nerd, half ninja.

THE RANCH

ON SATURDAY, MOM DRIVES
Carly and me to Calabasas and the
equine-therapy ranch. The woman
who started it is named Nancy; she
greets us at the top of the long
gravel road wearing cowboy boots

gravel

and the largest straw hat I've ever
seen. Mom and Nancy hug like old
friends.

Before Mom can introduce us,

barrage

overalls

mount

Carly starts in with a zillion questions, ranging from how many therapy horses Nancy has to what they eat and which horse is the tiniest. Nancy doesn't seem annoyed by the barrage of questions and answers every one. Carly's face lights up when a guy in overalls walks toward us with Maggie. She races to them, then realizes her mistake and slows down.

"I'm not sure how much time you've spent with horses," Nancy tells her, "but you should always approach, lead, and mount a horse from the left-hand side."

"That's from back when horses were used in battle," Carly says. "Soldiers mounted from the left so they could draw their swords on the right."

"What did left-handed soldiers do?" I ask.

My mother shakes her head and smiles. She's used to my weird questions by now. Carly also shrugs me off; she's too engrossed with Maggie to answer.

engrossed

The guy in the overalls introduces himself as Pete and asks if we want a tour of the stables. Mom and Nancy head inside to the office while Carly and I follow Pete down a dusty path toward a series of clapboard buildings.

clapboard

"We've got three acres," he explains. "We grow alfalfa on two of them to feed the horses. Miniatures have a lower metabolism than full-growns, so we have to be careful not to overfeed them. Believe it or not, obesity is a big problem with

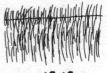

alfalfa

metabolism

these little guys." He turns to Carly and me. "You might be tempted to feed Maggie and the others today, but please don't. We really watch their diets."

"Even carrots?" Carly pulls out a bag from her backpack.

"Only if we cut them up and put them in her bucket," Pete answers. "I'm not a big believer in hand-feeding these babies. The last thing we want is for one of these horses to nip at someone at a hospital or nursing home."

Carly might be disappointed, but she takes rules too seriously to disregard them and slips the carrots back in her bag.

disregard

Each of the stables is divided into four stalls. The first one is occupied by miniature horses of different colors.

assortment

"We call these our assortment pack," Pete says. "We've got a black, a gray, a chestnut, and a white. Kids, meet Leonardo, Michelangelo, Donatello, and Raphael."

"Like the Ninja Turtles," I say. Before Carly can jump in, I add, "I know, I know; they were famous artists too."

Pete laughs. "The funny thing is, these horses are all females."

"But they COULD probably go down a sewer if they had to," I say. "They're definitely small enough to fit down a manhole."

manhole

Carly raises her eyebrow and shoots me the look she always does when she wants me to give it a rest.

"It's just about feeding time," Pete says. "You two want to help?"

Even though we won't be feeding them by hand, Carly and I jump at the chance. We top off their water and break up hay into the feed buckets.

Pete hands me a pitchfork. "You feel like mucking?"

pitchfork

Carly grabs the tool from his hand before I get to ask what mucking is— though I have a sneaking suspicion of what it might entail.

"Does that mean scooping poop?" I ask. It took me a long time to get used to picking up after Bodi; I don't need to clean up after horses too.

Carly, on the other hand, isn't bothered by the manure; within minutes, the floor of the stall is

manure

so clean you could eat off it. (I wouldn't—but Matt might.)

"Next, you can brush them," Pete says. "Daily grooming is important for horses—just like it is for humans."

I wonder if Mom fed any of these lines to Pete beforehand. Personal hygiene is one of Mom's pet peeves and something she gets on me for all the time. But brushing the hair of a miniature horse is a zillion times more fun than brushing your own.

peeves

Carly's in heaven grooming Maggie from head to tail while I focus on the Ninja Turtle horses. She uploads videos to Snapchat, VSCO, and Instagram demonstrating proper brushing technique and adds a photo of her and Maggie as #BFFs. I tell her to reel it in on the social

reel

media posting—though I'd be lying if I said I didn't make up a quick song on TikTok about the Ninja Turtles.

When we meet up with Nancy and Mom later, I think Carly's going to beg Mom to stay but she's relaxed, tranquil even, and thanks Nancy for the experience.

We say our good-byes and trek down the gravel road to the car. Mom stops at my favorite frozen yogurt place on the way home. She gets her usual—plain yogurt with strawberries—but Carly and I load up on gummy bears and M&M toppings. While we sit on the benches outside the shop to enjoy our treats, Carly asks Mom if we might be able to go back to Nancy's ranch sometime.

"That's what Nancy and I were

tranquil

talking about," Mom answers. "How'd you like to visit a few times a month and have it count for your community service hours at school?"

Carly's so excited, she practically knocks the cup of yogurt out of my hands. She already does community service helping her mother deliver Meals on Wheels to the elderly, and judging by the huge smile on her face, she'll be making room in her schedule for Maggie too.

"What about you, Derek?" Mom asks. "Nancy would also love to have you as a volunteer."

volunteer

"Sure." I keep my smile to myself. I'd never admit it, but I was secretly hoping Nancy's offer extended to me.

When we finish our yogurts, Mom starts the car and we catch the beginning of Carly's favorite Ariana Grande song. Carly sings along with so much energy that I end up joining in. Carly laughs in a way I haven't heard in months and it feels like normal Carly is back. I just hope the miniature-horse magic will last and she'll stay this way for good.

SUPERGIRL

FOR THE NEXT CODING CLASS, MS. Felix wants us to meet in the media center to do research. Most of us pretty much use our phones to look stuff up, but I don't think she trusts that we won't be doing other things like texting or playing games. (Lunch servers might have even better kid antennas than teachers do.)

It's a few minutes after the bell

hairnet

when Ms. Felix rushes through the media center's double doors with an armload of loose papers and her hairnet still stretched over her head. "Sorry I'm late." She clears her throat. "It's taken me all week to troubleshoot the problems with your student lunch balances. It's not often I get to be an IT consultant and a cafeteria lady at the same time."

Ms. Felix wants us to stay with the same partner we had last week, which means I'm still stuck with Jade instead of hanging out with Umberto. He's working with Sophie Hinton, who transferred to our school from London a few years ago and has an accent that makes Umberto swoon.

swoon

"It's not WHAT she says," he told

me last week. "It's HOW she says it that kills me. She sounds so elegant."

elegant

Sophie does seem pretty intelligent, but I think it has more to do with the fact that she has a memory like an encyclopedia than with her accent.

encyclopedia

Jade's already claimed a table in the back of the media center. The tabletop is covered with sheets of graph paper filled with her tiny scrawl. She barely looks up when she asks if I finished my part of the assignment.

claimed

"It took me eleven hours, but I did." I expect her to be happy with my accomplishment but she just nods and keeps working. Meanwhile, across the room, Sophie and Umberto are whispering and laughing like old friends.

scrawl

It seems as if every pair of partners has been able to bond over this assignment except Jade and me. Maddy and Emma created a babysitter app they are using to make extra cash. Nate and Leo made a haiku generator that has them in constant stitches with their random poems. How am I supposed to find out if Jade and I have anything in common when all we're making is a lame homework-organization app that I'll never use in a million years?

I wonder if I should make more of an effort to be personable with Jade, so I ask her if she's having a good week.

"I'm working on four major projects. I'm pretty tired," she answers.

"Four major projects besides this one?"

Hey. How are you?

Good. You?

personable

"This isn't a major project," she scoffs. "I did the work for this at breakfast."

So much for pride in my work. Jade must think I'm the slowest learner on the planet.

She points to my laptop and its almost-empty desktop files. "Aren't you going to write apps for that bad boy?"

I tell her I'm a long way from creating apps on my own.

She moves her laptop closer so I can see it. "I didn't like the queue in SoundCloud, so I wrote a program to improve it." She points to the songs in her playlist, none of which I've heard of. (Why am I not surprised?)

queue

"I can share it with you if you want," she adds.

I tell her I pretty much listen to

ridicule

hightails

music on YouTube, which causes her to grimace. Thankfully I'm saved from her ridicule when Ms. Felix tells us to take out our work so she can inspect it.

"I'll be right back," Jade says.

"Don't leave!" I say. "I can't explain this to Ms. Felix alone!"

"Calm down, I'll be two seconds." She hightails it toward the double doors while I pray Ms. Felix will save us for last.

After several minutes, I panic when I realize Ms. Felix is almost at our table. I'm about to push through the double doors to track down Jade but find her on the other side of a giant bookshelf sitting behind the librarian's desk. She's eyeing Ms. Myer's screen and typing something into her phone.

When I step into view, she flinches.

"Sorry, didn't mean to scare you."

"The only thing scary about you is how bad you are at Java." She tucks her phone in her back pocket. "I got so bored waiting for the librarian I almost hacked into her schedule to see when she'd be back."

I can't resist a rare opportunity to correct her. I explain to Jade that Ms. Myers goes home after the dismissal bell. "Coding class is AFTER school, remember?" It's nice to be ahead of Jade in at least ONE thing.

We slide into our seats just as Nate and Leo are reading one of their randomly generated haikus to the class:

flinches

Infected bathroom
A slimy butterfly sings
Despite the pudding.

Leo's laughing so hard he barely gets the words out. "Pudding in the bathroom!" he says. "The generator is so random!"

Ms. Felix smiles. "Good job." She turns her attention to my table. "Jade, Derek, you're up!"

I'm so nervous I nearly swallow my tongue. Thankfully, Jade does most of the talking.

snazzy

"It's a basic homework-organization app built on the frame-work of Evernote," she explains. "But with some snazzy modifications, of course."

Jade taps on one of the dates and a to-do list pops up. "You can input tasks and schedule an estimated amount of time for each." She double-taps an icon of a clock on fire. "There's also a race-against-the-clock feature that turns completing each assignment into a game. When you finish ahead of time, a party bus appears and unloads a colony of dancing penguins in sunglasses."

I didn't know our app did that!

Ms. Felix makes a few taps on Jade's keyboard to pull up the code input window for inspection:

colony

```
/* Method to check status
of assignment and start the
penguin celebration!
*/
public Boolean
celebrateCompletion(assignment){
    if (assignment.complete()){
```

```
         assignment.penguins.
celebrate();
         return true;
}
else{
         return false;
         }
}
```

pterodactyls

"There's also a reminder feature with screeching pterodactyls," Jade continues.

Every time Jade and I discussed our app it seemed boring, but seeing all these cool features in action is really selling me on the prospect of getting organized.

I can feel Ms. Felix waiting for me to contribute, so I say I programmed the dates and times. Ms. Felix gives us a thumbs-up, then heads to the front of the media center to pass out today's research assignment.

When I turn to thank Jade for doing all the heavy lifting, she barely notices because her fingers are flying across her keyboard. I ask what other stuff she's working on.

"There's always something to work on when you're a hacktivist," she says.

I ask her what on earth a hacktivist is.

activist

"An activist who hacks for the greater good," she answers.

"So you ARE a hacker!"

She shoots me a look to lower my voice.

"It's just another form of protest," she says. "Whenever a corporate overlord tries to crush the little guy."

Who IS this girl?

overlord

"But isn't that illegal?" I whisper.

"I never do anything for personal gain—just a little civil disobedience here and there." She stops typing and looks at me with a goofy grin. "My dad and I rerouted Waze so it thinks our street is one-way now. Cars used to fly through our neighborhood because Waze said it was a shortcut. Not anymore!"

disobedience

I've heard about activists sitting in trees so they won't get cut down or chaining themselves to fences to save a historic building from a wrecking ball, but I never realized there were people—and kids—using cyberspace to make the world a better place.

historic

Umberto's coding partner might have a cool British accent, but MY partner is a techie superhero!

CLASH OF THE TITANS

UNLIKE ME, CARLY IS NOT SO impressed with Jade's skills.

"What's wrong with protesting things IRL—with a placard and chants?" she asks. "I don't trust somebody who only slinks around on the Internet."

"I doubt she's slinking," I say. "Not with those boots anyway. All

placard

slinking

I know is we finished our project in no time." I turn to face Carly as she opens her locker. "I thought you said she was smart—or are you just envious that the entire school is obsessed with her apps?"

"I am not! And by the way—just a couple of weeks ago YOU were the one threatening to transfer to another school to get away from that Pirate Kittens theme song."

I can't deny Carly's comeback, so I keep my mouth shut. But it doesn't take long for her to start venting again. "She uses those cat ears and eyelash filters on Snapchat, so she's not the edgy rebel you think she is." She slams her locker closed. "I hate those stupid filters."

"OMG, you're stalking her on social

stalking

media! You told me you refused to follow her."

"Her stories are terrible," Carly answers. "And I'm not stalking!"

I don't think I've ever seen Carly this jealous before. I may be at the bottom half of my class in terms of grades, but I'm smart enough not to share that thought out loud with Carly.

I end up running into Jade several times during the day. As we walk to science, she tells me she's always loved technical stuff, that she used to rip open calculators in kindergarten just to play with the parts.

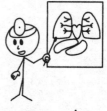

innards

"I love the innards of anything electronic," she continues. "I used to solder my brother's Matchbox

solder

cars and turn them into robots. My parents stopped me at alarm clocks, and even though I begged, microwaves were off-limits."

She tells me how her parents sneak her into DEFCON every year. I'm a little embarrassed that she has to explain what it is—a giant convention in Las Vegas for computer geeks. "You're supposed to be sixteen to attend," she says. "But my dad usually does a presentation, so I'm in, no questions asked."

Turns out Jade's parents are both in the software business, which explains her learning to code at such an early age. I guess it's similar to me being a natural cartoonist like my dad.

"My father invented software

that detects malware," Jade continues. "It's the best protection against computer viruses on the market."

detects

If I made a list of the smartest kids I know, Umberto and Carly would be at the top, but Jade is earning a place alongside them.

malware

When I tell her this, she shrugs. "I can't speak for your friends, but personally the whole prodigy thing is overrated. I just like working hard and staying busy."

prodigy

Jade waves me off and turns down the hall toward her classroom at the same moment that Matt tackles me outside science.

"You're turning into a full-fledged nerd," he teases. "Bags under your eyes, weird friends." He gestures toward Jade. "What's with her anyway? Seems like a snob."

I tell Matt that Jade is pretty much in her own little world.

"We all are," Matt responds. "And mine is riding skateboards after school. You in?"

I've been so busy writing code and making sure Carly's okay that I haven't been on my board in a while. I tell Matt I'll meet him at our usual spot at UCLA.

"Awesome. I invited Jason from my comedy class too. This kid's hilarious. Hope you don't mind."

"Oh, cool." But an unpleasant feeling washes over me as we part ways. Racing across UCLA as if it's our own personal skate park is a thing Matt and I have always done together. Why does it bother me so much that he invited someone else to join us this time?

At least my conversation with Jade today made me feel a little better about my coding skills. She's been surrounded by computer language since she was really young; she SHOULD be better than I am. It's like Charlie Hatfield having a dad who's a virtuoso guitarist; no one was surprised when Charlie won a national scholarship to a fancy guitar camp in fifth grade. Sometimes what you're good at comes from your family; sometimes you gravitate toward things because of your friends—which makes me even happier to be skateboarding with Matt tonight.

virtuoso

scholarship

gravitate

Even if he did invite a third wheel—I mean, a new friend.

MOUNT KILIMANJARO

SHE'S ONLY BEEN TO THE RANCH once but Carly's already on a mission to bring a few of the therapy horses to school. Nancy loves the idea and has a long phone conversation with Principal Demetri about the details. According to Carly, Nancy told him how the horses have visited other schools in our area with great success. Principal Demetri was hesitant until Carly shared how working with Maggie really helped quell her anxiety. Thanks to Carly's efforts—and honesty—Maggie and Leonardo will be attending school with us all day.

hesitant

"I can't remember the last time I was this excited," Carly says on our way in. "At another school Maggie went to, there was a girl who hadn't spoken in two years who suddenly leapt up and started speaking to Maggie. Talk about a miracle!"

quell

No one actually WAS talking about miracles. Still, Carly is so enthusiastic I don't want to burst her bubble.

But as soon as we walk through the front door of the school, something feels wrong—a weird combination of chaos and quiet.

If anyone will know what's going on, it's Matt, so we hurry down the hall. When we find him, he doesn't say a word, just points to his empty locker. "Every locker—in the ENTIRE school—is EMPTY!"

"Somebody stole all our stuff?!" My mind goes to the collectible Lakers jacket Dad got me that's been adorning the inside of my locker for months.

"That's the weird part," Matt continues. "Nothing was stolen." He walks us away from the rows of empty lockers to the gym. In the middle of the basketball court is a giant mountain of STUFF.

I can't help but think about how long it would take to write code for every single item in this pyramid of our possessions.

collectible

adorning

I run to the pile to pick out what's mine but Matt holds me back. "Demetri's putting a schedule together for each class to comb through the volcano of clothes and books," Matt says. "I already got a warning for trying to cannonball from the bleachers."

cannonball

Carly stares at the mound of sweaters, backpacks, and books. "What if our stuff is gone by the time our class gets to search through it? What if someone takes things that aren't theirs?"

"This must've taken all night." Matt shakes his head. "I can't decide if this is the best prank of all time or the worst."

As we discuss whether our soccer rivals across town would stoop this low, Carly suddenly grabs my arm.

rivals

"The horses are coming today—maybe they can help!"

"How?" asks Matt. "By eating the leftover lunches in that mountain of junk?"

Carly races to the office while Matt and I watch the confusion grow in the middle of the gym.

Umberto skids beside us. "There were lots of steps to pull this off. First, you'd have to get the combinations to every single locker."

Matt interrupts, "Our school has a supervillain!"

Umberto ignores him. "Then you'd have to have a shopping cart or something to haul everything to the gym."

"Or a wheelchair." Matt jokingly elbows Umberto.

"A wheelbarrow would work," I

say, getting the conversation back on track.

"Plus," Umberto continues, "you'd probably have to dismantle the security cameras." He wheels closer to the edge of the pile and takes it all in. "This was definitely not a one-person job. The kids who did this were pros."

dismantle

There are a few oohs and aahs when Carly escorts Nancy down the hall with Maggie and Leonardo. Natalie snaps a picture, then heads toward the gym.

Carly introduces Nancy to Matt and Umberto. "This is the perfect day to be here," Carly says. "I'm sure Maggie and Leonardo can help everyone deal with this."

Nancy doesn't seem so sure. "I don't know, Carly. I think kids might

recovering

scavenge

be preoccupied with recovering their property."

I watch Carly's face fall to the floor.

"Let's reschedule for another day," Nancy suggests. Carly nods and joins Nancy in leading the horses back outside.

When it's our class's turn to scavenge through the pile, I anxiously scan for the purple and gold of my Lakers jacket. That jacket cost my dad a bundle after last year's playoffs; I'm not sure how long I'll be able to pretend I lost it.

I'm relieved when Matt walks over wearing it. "Finders keepers," he says. "Good luck getting it back."

"You can wear it till tomorrow as a token of my appreciation," I answer. "Then it's mine."

token

I check in with Carly to make sure she's recovered all her things. I'm glad when she says everything is accounted for.

"It's too bad the horses didn't work out," I say. "Next time will be better."

"If there is a next time." Carly hangs her head and covers her face with her bangs the way she does when she doesn't want anyone to see she's upset.

We wait for the bus in silence, mostly because I don't want to say the wrong thing.

THE AFTERMATH

rampage

patrolling

trespassing

AFTER SUCH A MAJOR SECURITY breach, Principal Demetri goes on a rampage. There are suddenly two security guards patrolling the halls and announcements about new trespassing and vandalizing rules over the PA system several times a day.

"It's a war zone," Matt says. "I feel like any minute one of these guards is going to throw me against the wall and frisk me."

"It's not that bad," I respond. "But if the perpetrator's goal was to shake up the entire school, mission accomplished."

It also seems like the locker hijinks unleashed a tsunami of homework. Ms. Miller, Mr. Maroni, and Ms. McCoddle all give record amounts of assignments.

"If I ever find out who emptied our lockers, I'm going to stuff him in one myself," Matt says. "I've got three chapters to read for history tonight—thanks a lot, Mystery Prowler."

The rest of the week is spent with our heads buried in books—not my favorite place to be. By the time coding class comes around, my brain

frisk

perpetrator

hijinks

avalanche

admiral

presidential

is ready to explode in an avalanche of words and numbers.

"Today," Ms. Felix begins, "we're going to look at some of the contributions women have made to the field of computer science. Has anyone ever heard of Grace Hopper?"

Before Jade can raise her hand, Umberto does.

"She was a rear admiral in the navy and was awarded the Presidential Medal of Freedom."

I'm wondering what all this military stuff has to do with computer science when Jade chimes in. "She helped create the computer language COBOL in 1959 and invented one of the first linkers. Grace Hopper also made the first compiler—she even coined the term."

Judging from the looks around the room, it's safe to say I'm not the only one who has no idea what Jade is talking about. I raise my hand. "And in English that means...?"

"COBOL is 'COmmon Business Oriented Language,'" Ms. Felix explains. "It's been the standard programming language for large data mainframes since it was invented. And who can tell us what a compiler is?"

"It's a fancy word for translator," Jade says without raising her hand. "A compiler takes commands in one programming language and translates it into another. Like when you want to find out how to say things in French or Japanese."

Ms. Felix is impressed and tells us more about this naval officer who kicked butt in the computer world. "They called her Amazing Grace," Ms. Felix says. "She was a real pioneer in the field, building upon the first prototypes of program writing. And would you believe the person who conceived of the earliest code was also a woman—from the 1800s."

WHAT?!

"That's before computers were even invented!" I say.

din

"Crazy, right?" Ms. Felix cranks open one of the windows as she talks until the din of lawn mowers drowns her out. "Ada Lovelace is often referred to as the first computer programmer, although some say that her mentor, Charles Babbage, did most of the work."

Jade sighs loud enough for the

whole class to hear. "That always happens—people downplay the contribution of women."

downplay

Even though I've never heard of these women before, it's kind of cool they laid the groundwork for all the things we use computers and phones for today.

groundwork

"The work of these and other coders is the reason why every school has STEAM programs," Ms. Felix says. "It's important for you kids to realize how much power is in your hands but to also realize you're standing on the shoulders of giants."

I know Ms. Felix means that other people's efforts paved the way for the technology we use now, but the image of me standing on top of Andre the Giant as he fights John

paved

Cena is in my head for the rest of the day.

Ms. Felix gives us our next assignment—to create GIFs for the school's website. I lean back in my chair; I've been creating GIFs for years—piece of cake.

compression

"But here's the catch," she continues, "it's not the GIF I'm interested in. It's the compression."

Ohhhhhhhh.

Ms. Felix taught us about compression during our last class— how there's so much data in a program that you have to write ANOTHER program to make the data smaller. She wants us to work in the same pairs, which means Umberto and I will never get to team up. Jade rubs her hands together, probably excited at the prospect of doing something a little more challenging.

But I'm wrong.

"I automatically compress my files," she whispers, "so this assignment is pretty much done."

That's bad news in terms of learning, but good news in terms of my homework load. Her confession is music to my ears.

"Here's what we can do instead." Jade hands me a sheet of paper.

"I'm good. Thanks anyway."

But she still shoves the paper toward me. "Let's face it—Ms. Felix put us together because she knew you'd need help."

"She said that?"

"Just because I'm way ahead, I don't want to cheat you out of a learning opportunity. You can do this

instead. It's for the sequel to Pirate Kittens."

I tell her I already have plans to go to Dave & Buster's with Umberto this weekend. Then again, it WOULD be nice to have bragging rights on a game that's sure to sweep the school. I stare at the piece of paper and take Jade up on this bonus project—which will surely mean delaying my precious goof-off time.

"Hello? Earth to Derek?" Jade says. "You want to be a coder or not?"

The answer is yes. Yes, I do.

I tuck the page into my notebook and mentally gear up for several nights of work. Hopefully Umberto will understand.

SATURDAY BLUES

HERE'S A QUESTION—CAN YOU still call it a weekend if you spend every second working? Saturday starts off fine, with banana-pecan pancakes—thanks, Dad—and a Skype call to my grammy in Boston. Mom must've forwarded her pictures of Carly and me at the ranch, because Grammy asks if I'm going to visit the miniature horses again with "my

pecan

attentively

girlfriend." I tell my grandmother for the millionth time that Carly is NOT my girlfriend, but it's a one-sided joke she insists on telling whenever we talk. I love my grammy and listen attentively to her kidding around, but she needs to get some new material.

It turns out Carly IS at the ranch today. She bugged her mother so much that Mrs. Rodriquez carved out some time to drive to Calabasas so Carly could "introduce" them. She sends me a selfie with Maggie and Leonardo. I'd bet every dollar I ever got in a birthday card that Carly's asking Nancy if she can bring the horses to school again. That girl is like a dog with a bone when she gets an idea in her head.

The rest of the day is a repetition

repetition

of every other day this week. Numbers, letters, parentheses, greater-than symbols, less-than symbols, periods, underscores ... By dinnertime, I stare at the screen and can't decide if I spent the whole day working on something meaningful or pointless.

pointless

Dad hands me a plate of his famous chicken and dumplings. "Nice focus today! Very diligent!"

I nod and take a seat at the table.

diligent

Today was a lame excuse for a Saturday but having dumplings for dinner almost makes up for it.

Mom's at a "girls' night" at her friend Janine's so after dinner, Dad and I retire to the den for video games. Even though Mom loves it when Dad and I spend quality time together, she isn't keen on us staring at a TV while we do it. "There are so many other ways to have fun," Mom would say if she were here. But she's NOT here, so Dad and I settle onto the couch for a Fortnite marathon.

"We played for three hours!" Dad says later. "This game is a time suck!"

I hastily sweep all the cookie crumbs off the sofa, hoping our Couch Potato Time won't be too noticeable to Mom.

At school on Monday, I can't help but show off my hard work to Umberto. He runs his finger across the GitHub, studying my lines of code.

"This is for Pirate Kittens 2?" he asks. "It looks nothing like what she wrote for the first one. She's upping her game."

I kind of understand what Umberto's talking about but because I don't want to seem stupid—and don't feel like listening to a long answer if I ask him to explain—I just nod and say, "Yup."

revamp

"If this is what she's doing, I really have to revamp my program," Umberto says. "I spent so much time doing the compression assignment that Sophie and I hardly got to work on expanding our app."

If I DO end up going into computer programming, I hope missing out on the compression module won't impact my career. Who am I kidding—I got out of a big, boring assignment and got to work on a game with pirates instead!

When I see Jade outside the

gym, I open my laptop to show her all I did.

"I'll probably have to clean up the entire thing," she says as she scans my work.

accolades

Hardly the accolades I'd been hoping for.

"Good thing Ms. Felix is giving me extra credit for working with you."

"WHAT?"

Jade smiles. "Calm down. I'm kidding." She scans the lines of code and nods her head. "Not bad. If we eliminate some of the typos, this might actually run."

eliminate

Now THAT'S what I'm talking about.

Jade tells me the dates in the second section should be in chronological order but the rest looks pretty clean. "Good job. We might make a coder out of you yet."

chronological

Is it pathetic to admit how much I crave her approval? I spend the rest of the day walking on air, proud of myself for trying—and maybe succeeding—at something challenging and new.

ANOTHER MIX-UP

AS WE SKATEBOARD TO SCHOOL the next day, Matt pitches me ideas for his comedy class presentation.

"We're supposed to come up with an original character and give them a funny monologue," he explains. "I'm working on my impression of Jason's sister. She's a cheerleader at the high school who talks with a total Valley Girl accent that's just BEGGING to be made fun of."

He gives me a sample of his exaggerated teenage-girl voice. It's funny, but my laughter is forced. It sounds like Matt's been spending as much time with Jason as I have with Jade. Is learning to code going to end up costing me my best friend?

"I wonder if I'll find another note from my secret admirer today," Matt says when we hit a red light.

admirer

"You have a secret admirer?" *More importantly—how did I not know this?*

"I keep finding these purple papers in my locker," he says. "Little notes like 'Hope you're having a nice day.'"

"Sounds like something Carly would say."

"You don't think it's her, do you?" Matt asks. "I want it to be someone new."

"Maybe it's Jade. She's new."

"She's weird," Matt answers. "No, thanks."

We can tell from the top of the street that something's different at school today. "I hope it's not another locker break-in," Matt says. "When a prankster starts to repeat himself, it's time to throw in the towel and find a new line of work."

circular

When we reach the circular driveway, I figure out what's wrong. There are no buses anywhere. And hardly any kids.

"We're not early, are we?" Matt asks. "I can't damage my reputation by being early."

I check my phone and tell him we're on time. "Where is everyone?"

We ask a few kids who got dropped off but no one knows why school is currently a ghost town. Principal Demetri paces up and down the sidewalk, barking orders into his walkie-talkie.

"Is this a prank?" I ask Matt. "Or something more serious?"

A queasy feeling rises up inside me. Matt's eyes meet mine, and for once he doesn't have a snappy comeback.

queasy

We're both visibly relieved when Principal Demetri finally waves one of the buses into the parking lot. The bus driver looks as confused as our principal.

"Mrs. Sousa drove us to Brentwood!" Carly says when she gets off the bus. "Everyone was yelling that she was going the wrong way but she kept driving!"

anarchy

The shock on Matt's face continues to grow along with the chaos. "This is DEFINITELY the same person who raided the lockers! This is anarchy!"

"For a second I thought we were on some new reality show where we swap schools," Carly adds. "The whole thing was very stressful."

superintendent

Assistant Superintendent Menendez tries to clear the area around Umberto's van so he can safely get out. Matt, Carly, and I hurry over to help.

rerouting

When we press Mrs. Menendez for details, she tells us someone pretending to be the superintendent sent a five AM email rerouting the buses to another school. "The poor drivers were running all over town," she says. "Then parents calling in jammed the channels, so it took forever to let the bus drivers know the email was a hoax."

Since we're the first ones with the scoop, Matt races around the parking lot sharing the news with the rest of the school. Carly seems overwhelmed by the commotion and heads inside.

Umberto gives my sleeve a tug. "Do you know how hard it would be to hack into the school district's computers to send an email from the superintendent? Not to mention the logistics of rerouting dozens of buses."

The queasiness in my stomach returns.

"There are a handful of people

who have the computer skills to pull that off," he continues. "And one of them is someone we know."

I shake my head. "No way."

"Yes way," Umberto says and nods his head. "Jade."

"Maybe TECHNICALLY she's capable, but why? When she talked about being a hacktivist, she said she only did things that HELPED people."

havoc

Umberto looks around; it's going to be a while before school will start today. "Maybe Jade's bored with coding games and wants to create havoc instead." He takes off his Dodgers hat and scratches his head. "You have to talk to her, Derek. You're the one who knows her best."

confront

"You want me to confront

someone who might've orchestrated this giant mess? Thanks, but no thanks."

"Just talk to her and see what you can find out," Umberto says. "Because I'm talking to Demetri."

Umberto wheels inside to join Carly, leaving me completely unsure of what to do. On the one hand I'm glad no one was hurt in today's hacking prank, but these stunts are getting bigger. Who knows what the next one could be? On the other hand, the last thing I want to do is antagonize my lab partner, who's spared me from several difficult assignments.

antagonize

Jade couldn't be behind this chaos, could she?

THE HARSH TRUTH

blunder

THE REST OF THE MORNING IS one blunder after another. The superintendent visits the school but gets caught in the gridlock of the rerouted buses. Mr. Demetri doesn't realize the PA is still on and lets out a curse word for all to hear. The only one who seems amused by the confusion is Jade, snapping her gum and twirling a new plastic wristband.

"Were you dumpster diving at the hospital last night?" I ask. "Or were you up to a different kind of mischief?"

"Like what?" She twirls her locker open with the speed of a safecracker. "Making my pet monkey jump out of the laundry basket?"

safecracker

Before I can answer, she tells me she spent last night watching my old YouTube videos. Her comment makes me miss Frank more than I already do, but I stay focused and forge ahead.

"I was thinking about something more malicious," I whisper. "Like hacking into the school's server."

malicious

Her face remains passive but

I notice a flicker in her eyes. "You think I'm the one who rerouted the buses?"

hypothetically

"I'm not the only one. So does Umberto." I dig in my heels. "And he's planning to rat you out."

"Let's say, hypothetically, you were right." She guides me down the hall away from the other students. "Suppose I DID hack into the district's server. Wouldn't I need help?"

I shake my head. "You could do it alone. You're THAT good."

accomplice

Jade seems pleased. "Thank you." She reaches into her parachutist backpack and takes out a piece of paper. "But if I DID hack into the server, wouldn't it be more fun to do it with an accomplice? Especially an unwitting one."

unwitting

I stare at the page in her hand and recognize my code.

"You said we were working on Pirate Kittens 2." My throat closes up; I can barely breathe.

"If anybody rats me out, they'll discover YOU wrote as much of that bus-route code as I did. The locker heist too. Unfortunately, there's no way to program a wheelbarrow—I was up all night emptying every locker by hand."

heist

"Are you telling me I helped write the code for these pranks?" My mouth hangs open as my mind races to Umberto—hopefully he hasn't had his chat with Demetri yet.

"How did you get into the server?" I ask.

"Easy. Every school librarian has access, and Ms. Myers keeps all her passwords on a sticky note stuck to her desk drawer."

I gasp. "THAT'S what you were doing when I caught you behind her desk last week?"

She nods. "Our next mission is to hack into everyone's grades."

"WE don't have a mission!" I shout. "Count me out."

"Like it or not, we're in this together," Jade says.

expelled

I race down the hall toward the office before Umberto gets me expelled.

I can't believe it. I've been hacked!

WHAT DO I DO NOW?

WHEN I SPOT UMBERTO ROLLING down the hallway, I grab ahold of his wheelchair and ask if he already spilled the beans to Demetri. Luckily, he was waylaid by Sophie on route to Demetri's office and didn't get a chance to share his theory about Jade yet.

waylaid

"Remind me to send Sophie a thank-you card." I sigh with relief.

"Is everything okay?" Umberto asks.

I can't tell if it's nerves, but I suddenly feel like everyone's eyes are on me. "I'll tell you at lunch." I turn my gaze to the floor and walk to my next class as casually as possible.

Sitting in science, I'm so upset I barely catch a word of today's

conductivity

lecture on conductivity. How could I have been so stupid to blindly follow Jade's instructions without spending the extra time to UNDERSTAND them? Jade was smart enough to realize I'd do almost anything to get out of work, so she played me like a finely tuned fiddle. Making me part of her plan to disrupt the school was a surefire way to ensure I couldn't turn her in.

During lunch, I call an emergency meeting with my friends in the corner of the cafeteria.

"Why can't we sit at our usual table?" Matt asks. "Jason was going to run through his new stand-up act."

I feel another twinge of regret but I've got bigger problems to think about right now than somebody encroaching on best-friend territory.

regret

"You were right," I tell Umberto. "Jade's the one responsible for rerouting the buses, setting everyone's lunch balances to zero, AND breaking into all the lockers."

encroaching

"I told you she was trouble!" Carly

whispers. "I never trusted her from day one."

"The Girl in Black?" Matt asks. "I knew she was weird but didn't think she was such a criminal mastermind!"

mastermind

I take a deep breath; this part of the story is much less fun to admit than the first part. "Uhmm, I kind of helped her write the code that got her everyone's locker combinations and rerouted the buses."

Carly and Matt seem confused but Umberto gets it right away.

inadvertently

"Did you deliberately help her?" he asks. "Or inadvertently?"

I'm not sure what *inadvertently* means but I tell Umberto I didn't help Jade on purpose. "We've been partners for weeks; she does most of the work and I do the smaller parts she gives me."

Umberto shakes his head. "It's actually a pretty genius plan—you can't turn her in because you helped write the code."

"But WE can turn her in," Matt says. "There's no way she's pinning this on you. I'm finding Demetri."

Matt gets up and grabs his tray, then Carly yanks him back into his seat. "If we turn Jade in, we turn in Derek too. We need a better plan."

Umberto moves his fork around his baked ziti, clearly upset. "I saw the code you wrote. I should've caught it."

ziti

"This isn't on you, Umberto—it's on me. I'm the one trying to skate by on minimal work."

"We ALL try to skate by on

minimal work!" Matt says. "That's what being in school IS."

Carly rolls her eyes and tells Matt to speak for himself. "The four of us are smarter than she is," Carly says. "We can fix this."

"That's nice of you to say but hardly true," I answer.

"There's no way she'll get away with this," Carly continues. "My house—after school. Operation Save Derek begins."

As foolish as I feel for letting myself get caught in this scheme, it's nice knowing I've got three friends who have my back every single time I need it—which unfortunately is a lot.

OVER OUR HEADS

WE ALL MEET UP AT CARLY'S—
even Umberto, who had to finagle an
excuse with his van driver. "I told him
we had a last-minute crisis with an
assignment," Umberto says, "which
technically is kind of true."

Carly brings out a plate of
her usual nutritious snacks: cut-
up carrots, celery, and hummus.
I'd rather have the cookies and

finagle

nutritious

licorice from my house but I'm not going to complain since everyone is dropping what they're doing to help me out.

preliminary

"Here's the thing I'm worried about," Umberto begins. "Suppose the lockers, the lunch balances, and the buses were preliminary hacks—just to see what she could get away with. Suppose she's got her eyes on something bigger?"

"Like what?" Matt scoops a wad of hummus with his celery and slurps it off. Carly pulls the bowl away.

hassle

"If she got into the district servers, she could access teacher information," Umberto says. "She could hassle people online, steal their identities—all kinds of nasty things."

We talked about cyberbullying in

Mr. Ennis's YouTube class last year; it's a serious offense and makes me afraid for what else Jade has up her hospital-bracelet sleeves.

offense

"Grades," Derek says.

"Grades," Umberto echoes. It makes perfect sense. She's already hacked into the district server. She could start selling A's to the highest bidder."

bidder

"We have to stop her," Carly adds.

"Whoa, let's not get ahead of ourselves," Matt says. "Making A's available to every student seems very democratic to me—almost a public service."

NEXT
PRESIDENT

MAN 7%
WOMAN 93%

democratic

"I know I'm the LAST person who should weigh in on this, but instant A's do sound tempting," I suggest.

Carly crosses her arms. "Derek,

I know you helped her accidentally, but whose side are you on now?"

"Yours!" I continue. "Jade even admitted she plans on hacking grades."

"She TOLD you what she's doing and you forgot to tell us?" Carly cries.

"It's not that I forgot..."

Matt shakes his head. "Part of you WANTS her to hack into our grades, because your grades have nowhere to go but up."

I'm embarrassed to admit it, but Matt is 100 percent correct.

"Derek, come on," Umberto says. "That would be every shade of wrong and you know it."

vital

Carly seems almost wounded that I held back this vital piece of information, so I throw out something to get back in her good graces.

"I've been giving this a lot of thought," I begin, "and I think the best thing to do is for me to come clean and tell Demetri everything— even if I get in trouble too."

"I doubt you'll get expelled if you tell the truth," Umberto says. "Honesty is the best policy."

"Derek!" Matt interrupts. "You've gotten out of worse scrapes than this! You're my hero! You caught a graffiti vandal, you did stunts in a movie, you solved the mystery of a babysitter who drowned, you had a monkey!"

"I LOST a monkey too," I say. "That hardly counts as an accomplishment." But I am happy to hear Matt call me his hero. His vote of confidence in my skills—especially when he's been spending so much time with a new friend—is the only piece of good news in this whole mess.

Matt stands up and crosses his arms. "We're ninjas, remember? What would Sensei Takai say?"

I smile at the memory of our super-tough martial arts teacher.

Carly sighs. "For once, I agree with Matt. You GOT this."

musketeers

"WE'VE got this." Umberto puts out his hand in an "All For One And One For All" Three Musketeers handshake. Even though there are four of us instead of three, our bond seems just as strong.

unanimous

But even with my friends' unanimous support, I still have no idea how to proceed with bringing Jade to justice.

"I know this sounds petulant," Carly begins.

"It doesn't, because none of us knows what that means," Matt interrupts.

petulant

Carly ignores him. "I think it's time Jade gets a taste of her own medicine."

"Am I hearing you correctly?" I pretend to bang the wax out of my ears. "Are you saying we should hack Jade?"

"Not necessarily. I just think being on the receiving end of one of these pranks might be the best way for Jade to learn her lesson." A sneaky smile creeps across Carly's face. "And it WOULD be kind of fun."

"There are a few things we could do, while still staying inside the law." Umberto rubs his hands together like he's been waiting for permission to unleash a sinister plan. "And now that we know what she's up to, we can set a trap to catch her red-handed."

"If we're going to be hatching an evil scheme," Matt says, "we DEFINITELY need some sugar."

"It IS the best brain food," I add. Matt and I share a nod. This situation is far from ideal but I'm happy to know so much time apart hasn't done our friendship any damage.

Carly runs to the kitchen for more snacks. When she returns, the four of us settle down to come up with a great—and legal—way to get back at Jade.

SHOWTIME

IT TURNS OUT THAT SOPHIE Hinton has been the one leaving notes in Matt's locker, which bums out Umberto but makes Matt's day.

"I can't believe it," Umberto complains. "My coding partner was after Matt this whole time. I guess it's true what they say—girls will always take a sense of humor over brains."

international

"The best part is now whenever I get her notes, I can read them in an English accent," Matt says. "I can't believe I have an international girlfriend."

"She's not your girlfriend!" Carly, Umberto, and I shout.

"Besides, we've got more important things to worry about," I continue. "Like saving me from getting kicked out of school."

"If we stick to our plan, we'll be fine," Umberto says. "Any questions?"

"I have one." I scan the faces of my three friends. "Is anyone else scared?"

uncharted

"We'd be crazy NOT to be scared," Carly announces. "This is uncharted territory for all of us. I barely slept last night."

Matt lets out an evil whisper. "It's GO time."

"We're not in a heist movie," Carly says. "Enough with the snarky dialogue—we've got work to do."

snarky

"Which is just another line of snarky dialogue." Good old Matt—he always has to have the last word.

"Stop bickering," Umberto inter-rupts. "If we're going to pull this off, we need to cooperate. Operation Save Derek is now in effect." He races down the hall to implement Phase One of the plan.

bickering

As fun as pretending to be spies has been these past few days, I'm still not sure we're doing the right thing. I lay in bed last night for hours debating whether or not to tell my parents everything. I know they'd want me to tell Demetri; they

dismay

shortcut

might even call him directly. Both of them would understand that Jade framed me, but when I pictured the looks of disappointment on their faces, I couldn't bring myself to tell them. I've seen their expressions of dismay before, and even though I was involved with these pranks accidentally, it would all come down to the fact that I was trying to take a shortcut with my work—again. If I were a superhero, trying to get out of work would be my fatal flaw, the same way Supergirl avoids Kryptonite.

In the end, I decide to figure this out with my friends and leave spilling the beans to my parents as plan B. Besides, now isn't the time to procrastinate. For once, it's time to ACT.

D-DAY

MY PHONE DINGS IN MY POCKET; it's Jade telling me to meet her after second period. I've been mentally preparing for this moment but seeing Jade's text makes it real. A bolt of fear shoots up my spine.

Jade called last night to review all the details of her master plan. As soon as we hung up, I group-texted Matt, Umberto, and Carly

counterattack

to update them and make sure our counterattack would still be effective.

The bell rings after world history. I take a deep breath and make my way to the door. *Act natural.*

"Derek?"

Ms. McCoddle's voice nearly makes me jump out of my skin. "Can you do me a favor and deliver this projector to the kindergarten room? Ms. Tatreaux asked to borrow it and I know her classroom is on your way." Ms. McCoddle smiles and nudges the projector cart toward me.

What do I do? I'm supposed to meet Jade outside the main office right now—there's no way I can do both.

"Sorry, Ms. McCoddle," my mouth

starts speaking before I have my excuse lined up. "But I—"

"I'll do it," Carly says from the doorway. "I love visiting the kindergartners."

Quick thinking, Carly. What would I do without you?

Once we make it to the hallway, I tell Carly I owe her one. She shakes her head and tells me to find Jade.

My hacker lab partner doesn't waste time on pleasantries when I find her outside the main office. "So the program I—we—wrote disables the security camera in Demetri's office at ten o'clock," she begins. "The master file with all the grades can only be accessed through Demetri's computer, so as soon as

pleasantries

thumb drive

I gain access, you download the file onto this thumb drive."

She hands me a flash drive the same shade of blue as my skateboard. What I'd give to be shredding down a half pipe right now instead of getting ready to break into the principal's office.

An alarm goes off on her phone, letting us know it's ten o'clock.

"I wrote the program to activate then because the administrators have a meeting with the assistant superintendent about the bus thing," Jade explains.

I have no idea how Jade knows so much about the comings and goings of the school; I can barely keep track of my own schedule, never mind anyone else's.

We both pretend to be opening

lockers when Demetri walks by with Assistant Superintendent Menendez and the rest of the office staff.

"Somebody will stay behind to answer phones," I whisper.

Jade shakes her head. "It's a mandatory meeting. The calls will go straight to voice mail." She slips into the office, holding the door so I won't chicken out. She points to the red light on the security camera in the corner of Demetri's office, which is usually green. "No one will even know we were here."

beeline

She makes a beeline to Demetri's desk. When she gets to his computer, her fingers race across the keyboard. I try to distract myself from how nervous I am by looking at the photos next to Demetri's computer.

skiff

"I didn't know Principal Demetri was a sailor." I pick up the framed picture of our principal waving aboard a skiff with a small, floppy-eared wiener dog in his arms. Jade tells me to stop touching things.

I carefully set the photo down and shove my hands in my pockets. I immediately clench the flash drive. Suppose something goes wrong? Suppose I actually help her steal the grades of every student that goes here? Does our plan actually MAKE me a criminal? Then I spot something that makes my entire body collapse with relief. I tap Jade on the shoulder.

"What?" she snaps.

The light on the security camera is now a bright, steady green.

"What's going on here?" Principal

Demetri suddenly appears in the doorway. His arms are crossed and I can tell he's having a difficult time remaining calm. Behind him are Umberto, Matt, and Carly.

"There's no way my program had a mistake," Jade says. "I checked it a hundred times."

"You wrote a program that turned off the camera at ten," I answer. "But I wrote a program that turned it back on at ten-oh-five—with a little help from Umberto."

"Principal Demetri didn't believe us when we told him one of his own students was responsible for these hacks," Umberto tells her, "but then we told him he'd be able to catch you in the act."

He hands me my new trusty laptop to really rub it in Jade's face:

```
// settings for camera
HashMap<String, Boolean>
settings = {active: true};
// log in to camera, update
settings
public void update _
camera(settings, user){
        if(user.auth == true){
                for(int i = 0; i
< settings.length(); i++){
                        camera.
settings[i] = settings[i];
                }
        }
}
update _ camera(settings, Jade);
```

cucumber

Jade stays cool as a cucumber as my friends and I reveal we've been one step ahead of her. I wasn't expecting Jade to burst into tears or anything, but she should at least be ANNOYED that we foiled her plan.

I think she's finally about to react when she turns to me and holds out the steadiest palm I've ever seen.

"Derek, may I please have my flash drive back?"

She stares at me, not blinking, until I hand it over.

"Jade, you're in a lot of trouble. We're calling your parents." Principal Demetri leads us into the hall, not letting Jade out of his sight. He looks at all of us and his eyes land on me. "Good job getting to the bottom of this. I won't forget that you had the school's best interests at heart." He nods for us to head to class, then closes his office door.

"We should totally get some free passes out of this," Matt says as we head down the hall. "Today is worth three or four major screwups for sure."

"That girl is fearless," Umberto said. "She didn't even break a sweat."

Matt shakes his head. "She's got to be half robot or something. No wonder she's so good at computers."

"A digital mastermind," Carly says. "Who WE outsmarted."

framed

I stop dead in my tracks. "Did I just go from a victim who got framed to the guy who saved the school?"

Carly bats her eyes and clutches her chest. "My hero."

Even though she's kidding, right now I feel like one.

I wrote a computer program that saved the school!

YOU'RE KIDDING, RIGHT?

IT'S A GOOD THING I WASN'T expecting a parade to celebrate my victory because hardly anyone found out how I rescued our school from a giant hack. Demetri wanted to keep the whole Jade affair hush-hush, so there weren't a lot of congratulations coming my way. I did end up filling in my parents— with the expected results.

victory

congratulations

"Why didn't you tell us WHILE this was going on?" Mom asks. "We're always here for you—you know that!"

"I wonder if the police will get involved," Dad says. "Maybe even the feds."

"Nothing would make me happier than if they throw the book at Jade," I add. "In fact, I'd like to be the one to throw it."

It takes me a while to convince them that everything is fine, mostly by steering the conversation to my new skills. I take my laptop from my bag and open it to the desktop.

sprinkling

The screen now has a sprinkling of applications.

Mom's hand flies to her mouth in shock.

"Look at all these apps." Dad scans the screen. "Even a homework scheduler."

"For all her flaws, Jade DID create some pretty cool programs," I add.

Mom opens each of the folders one by one, praising Jade's—and my—work. I know what she's going to say before she even opens her mouth, so I beat her to the punch.

"I'm not giving up on coding because of the Jade mess," I tell my parents. "A lot of what Ms. Felix said makes sense—I want to be able to contribute to the digital world, not just stare at it from the sidelines."

"Well, that was worth the price of the computer right there." Dad smiles.

To celebrate, Mom makes my favorite treat—she slices a pint of vanilla ice cream with an electric knife and stuffs the cutout circles between two warm chocolate chip cookies. A homemade ice cream sandwich that's a gooey, delicious mess.

homemade

Outside the cafeteria the next day, I stop dead in my tracks when I spot Jade.

"What are YOU doing here?" I ask. "I thought you got expelled!"

"Remember when I told you my dad was a computer consultant?"

"Uhm . . . yeah."

"Well, his specialty is cyber-security. Companies hire him to see if he can find a breach in their systems."

"Thanks for sharing, Jade, but I

don't really care about your father's job right now."

She shakes her head with an expression that tells me she's waiting for me to catch up. "My father was hired by the L.A. Unified School district."

unified

"So he must be furious that his own daughter was trying to change people's grades!"

She stares at me like I'm a dolt, and I'm beginning to feel like one.

dolt

Jade's arms flail wildly in the air. "Hel-lo! I was helping my dad discover where the breaches were in the system!"

flail

WAIT, WHAT?

"I was looking for holes in the school's firewall," she continues. "And I did a pretty good job, don't

firewall

scamming

you think? The district's servers were ripe for the picking. Look how many times I got in."

Is she scamming me again? There's no way she was working FOR the school this whole time.

"Not even Principal Demetri knew the city hired my father," she continues. "At my last school, I hacked into the sprinkler system and set the cafeteria sprinklers to go off during lunch. It was totally *Cloudy with a Chance of Meatballs*."

"As fun as a soggy food fight sounds, you were still causing trouble and costing the school money."

Jade crinkles her nose. "My dad IS furious with me. I'm supposed to just *tell* him if I find any breaches, not *act* on them. Between setting off the sprinklers at my last school and rerouting the buses here, I'm grounded for the rest of the year."

"Welcome to my world."

"Demetri put me on probation and gave me fifty hours of community service. I'm not a bad person—but I find it tempting to cause trouble when no one's looking. I guess I'm having a hard time keeping myself in check."

probation

"If you're looking for advice in making good choices, you're talking to the wrong guy," I say. "It's a struggle every day, ten times a day."

"I was really tempted to send McCoddle emails from your account asking for tutoring help on the weekends," Jade says.

"Am I supposed to thank you for

not making my life more miserable than you already did?"

"The good news is you're not a tourist anymore," she continues. "You can be someone who contributes to the Internet, not just takes from it."

chide

"Says the girl who's always glued to her phone," I chide.

Jade shrugs. "Getting sucked into a rabbit hole versus making conscious choices is a battle for all of us."

"The Internet in a nutshell," I agree.

She pulls her phone out of her pocket and heads down the hall as her thoughts surround me. When it comes to the Internet, will I be part of the problem? Or part of the solution?

A PICTURE WORTH A THOUSAND WORDS

THE NEXT DAY, CARLY STOPS ME outside of school and tells me she has a surprise to cheer me up after the recent uproar.

uproar

"You didn't have to get me anything," I tell her. "I'm just glad all this is over."

"You were there for me when I really needed it," she says. "Now it's my turn to take care of YOU."

Knowing what she's probably got in store, I tell her I don't have time to go to Calabasas and hang out with the ninja horses this week.

"Then I guess the ninja horses will have to come to you." Carly opens the front door of the school as if she's a woman highlighting prizes on an old TV game show.

highlighting

Inside, Nancy and Pete are holding the miniature ninjas—plus Maggie—in the center of a large circle of students.

"This time there's no drama to diminish the superpower of miniature horses!" Carly says. As soon as Maggie sees Carly, Maggie trots over for a nuzzle.

diminish

"Just two mammals getting mushy over each other." Matt comes up behind me and sticks his finger down his throat as if he's about to puke.

"Don't worry—I doubt Sophie will get jealous." Carly steps aside and motions for Matt to come closer. "Come on—Maggie loves it when you pet her neck."

Matt rolls his eyes but Carly doesn't budge, and after a moment he tentatively reaches out his hand to pet Maggie. He pulls his hand back quickly when Maggie turns her head.

tentatively

"You're AFRAID!" I say. "That's why you've been making fun of us this whole time!"

"I'm not scared of this little pony!" Matt says. "My bike is bigger than her!"

As if Maggie can understand what he's saying, she swings around

reins

quickly to face Matt, who jumps back five feet.

"You ARE afraid!" Carly laughs as she reins in Maggie.

Matt's cheeks turn as red as a Santa Monica sunset. I fake-punch him in the arm and tell him it's okay to be frightened of a horse the size of a Chihuahua. He's about to punch me for real when Umberto wheels himself between us.

"Matt, knock it off or I'll tell Sophie not to send you any more love notes," Umberto says.

Matt composes himself immediately, more afraid of losing his admirer than of a horse.

Carly points out Maria, a girl on the yearbook committee who's snapping pictures of students and teachers posing with the horses. "Maria is following the horses around all day. They might even get their own page in the yearbook."

Since most people use their phones to take pictures, it's odd to see Maria documenting the occasion with a clunky camera. I'm not sure I'd feel comfortable using one, but Maria is pretty smart, so I figure she knows how to operate such a complicated gizmo.

gizmo

As Maria snaps pictures of kids interacting with the horses, I realize Carly was right—these therapy horses really do light people up from the inside. After all the bedlam our school's been through, the calming presence of the horses offers everyone some much-needed relief.

bedlam

The last person I want to see amid all this calm is Jade, but sure enough, she's posing with Maggie and the ninja horses too. When she

outskirts

spots me on the outskirts of the group, she waves as if nothing ever happened and walks over.

"Adorable, right?" she says. "I totally missed them last time."

"Oh, because you were absent that day from being up all night ransacking our lockers?"

Jade looks at me and smiles. "Don't take it personally."

"It DOES seem like working with your dad is a pretty fun job."

"Especially when you get to prank a friend in the process."

"We are SO not friends," I answer.

Jade fake-frowns. "Then why do I know so much about you?"

"Uhm...because you hacked my phone?"

"Oh, THAT'S why." She flashes me a goofy grin and for a moment

I see a universe where Jade and I CAN be friends.

"I have to admit, I DID feel kind of empowered writing that code with Umberto to turn the security camera back on."

empowered

"There's hope for you yet, Derek Fallon." Jade slips her phone into her pocket. "See you in coding class."

"I don't get the wearing-all-black thing," Matt says as he watches her go. "But you have to admit, she IS kind of cool."

"Not as cool as Sophie Hinton," I respond.

"You got that right." Matt smiles. "We're going to the movies on Saturday." Matt suddenly pulls me down the hall where Maria is photographing the miniature horses in front of the school's trophy cabinet. "Do they give out trophies for best pooper?" Matt laughs.

No one can spot a poop-joke faster than Matt; it is actually one of his superpowers. Sure enough, Raphael lets out several road apples onto the tiled floor. Everyone laughs except for Nancy and Pete, who remain calm.

"As the picture book says— 'everybody poops.' Even creatures as adorable as these." Pete takes out a large waste bag from the back pocket of his jeans. But instead of picking up the waste, he sets his gaze on me.

"Hey, Derek," he calls. "You still afraid of mucking?"

That's all Matt has to hear. "NOW look who's scared," he teases.

"I'm not afraid—I just don't want to!"

"Sure." Then my best friend leads a chant and everyone in the hall immediately joins in. Dozens of my classmates are now clucking like chickens, taunting me to pick up after Raphael.

clucking

"Really, Matt?" I say. "Very mature."

"Don't you mean 'manure'?" he teases.

offending

The chanting shows no signs of letting up, so I grab the plastic bag from Pete and remove the offending clumps just as Maria snaps a photo. She immediately laughs, passing the camera for everyone to check out the picture.

"I think we just found the cover for the yearbook," Maria says.

"His face is so scrunched up you can barely tell it's Derek," Matt says. "I think you should enlarge it to poster size."

I hand over the bag of humiliation to Pete, who takes it outside to the dumpster. "I thought that miniature horses were supposed to take away stress, not add more," I complain to Carly. "Bringing them here was a TERRIBLE idea."

slideshow

Carly asks Maria if she can borrow her camera, then scrolls through its memory, giving me a slideshow of my classmates' happy faces.

embrace

"This has been a rough month," Carly confesses. "Ms. Costa helped me realize how much pressure I put on myself. I'm trying to embrace my mistakes instead of thinking it's the end of the world when I make one."

"I could have told you mistakes aren't the end of the world," I say. "I make so many every day, I have no choice but to accept them."

"When you and Umberto were talking about coding a few weeks ago, you said something that really helped."

"I did?!"

Carly laughs. "Now that I think about it, it was probably Umberto."

"Very funny."

"You said there were lots of different ways to program something—not just one way to reach your goal."

"I think that WAS me," I say.

Carly gives me a fake shove. "I

always thought there was one way to do things—but there are lots of ways to move forward. Learning that and talking to Ms. Costas helped me turn things around."

Am I hearing things or did I actually help Carly process a new piece of information? Maybe the deeper human goals Ms. Felix was talking about are possible after all.

Matt runs over and grabs the camera, pointing to the last picture of me in the slideshow. "You look like an idiot. I hope no one makes a meme out of it."

"Excellent idea." Umberto wheels over. "Maria, make sure to forward me that picture, okay?"

I am the butt of the joke again—literally—which means things are

pretty much back to normal, even
after all the trouble with Jade.

Except for one crucial difference:

crucial

```
public class Success{
     public static void
main(String[] args){
          System.out.println("I
KNOW HOW TO CODE!");
     }
}
```

I KNOW HOW TO CODE!

Acknowledgments

A BIG THANK-YOU TO KIERA PALTZ FROM The Coding School in Studio City, California, for sharing her expertise, as well as letting me meet with some of her fabulous students—Zoe Winston, Alan Shaaban, Calvin Colker, and Sebastian Tyner. The Coding School teaches students all around the country to code via Skype and workshop classes with their wonderful teachers, of which Greg Garnhart was especially helpful. It was a joy to talk to such dedicated teachers and students about one of the most critical subjects being taught in schools today. I learned so much!

My Life as a Book

Derek Fallon has trouble sitting
still and reading. But creating cartoons
of his vocabulary words comes easy.
If only life were as simple!

My Life as a Stuntboy

Derek gets the opportunity of a lifetime—
to be a stuntboy in a major movie—
but he soon learns that it's not as
glamorous as he thought it would be.

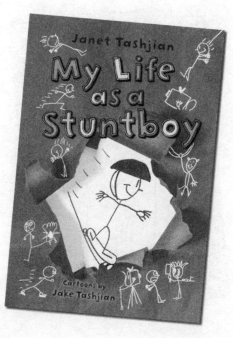

My Life as a Cartoonist

There's a new kid at school who
loves drawing cartoons as much
as Derek does. What could be better?

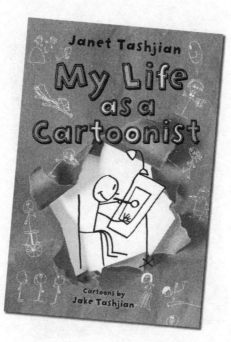

My Life as a Joke

Now in middle school, Derek just wants to feel grown-up—but his own life gets in the way, and he feels more like a baby than ever.

My Life as a Gamer

Derek thinks he's found his calling when he's hired to test software for a new video game. But this dream job isn't all it's cracked up to be!

My Life as a Ninja

Derek and his friends are eager to learn more about ninja culture. When someone starts vandalizing their school, these ninjas-in-training set out to crack the case!

My Life as a Youtuber

Derek becomes a popular Youtuber just as his foster capuchin, Frank, must go off to monkey college, so Derek furiously scrambles to find a reason for Frank to stay. What if Frank became a part of his Youtube videos?

My Life as a Meme

Adventures in dog-sitting for the Instagram-famous Poufy propel Derek to more Internet spotlight. He is finally a viral meme, but it's not long before his fame spins out of control!

About the Author

Janet Tashjian is the author of many best-selling and award-winning books, including the My Life series, the Einstein the Class Hamster series, the Marty Frye, Private Eye series, and the Sticker Girl series. Other books include *The Gospel According to Larry*, *Vote for Larry*, and *Larry and the Meaning of Life* as well as *Fault Line, For What It's Worth, Multiple Choice*, and *Tru Confessions*. She lives in Los Angeles, California.
janettashjian.com • mylifeasabook.com

author

About the Illustrator

Jake Tashjian is the illustrator of the My Life series and the Einstein the Class Hamster series. He has been drawing pictures of his vocabulary words on index cards since he was a kid and now has a stack taller than a house. When he's not drawing, he loves to surf, read comic books, and watch movies.
jaketashjian.com

illustrator